The Dragon Codex

Quest for the Relics of Design

In a realm where dragons, magic, and design intertwine, a dark force threatens the kingdom's very existence. It's up to Draco, Lumi, and Arka to embark on a daring quest to unravel this mystery.

As they journey through the land, they must hone their graphic design and artistic skills to save their world from impending doom.

By David Block

Dedication

In loving memory of Jordan Kaitlyn Block

February 17, 1999 - May 2, 2024

On May 2nd, 2024, we tragically lost our daughter, Jordan Kaitlyn Block, in a sudden and heartbreaking event. This book is dedicated to honoring and celebrating her life and the immense impact she had on everyone around her.

Jordan was an amazing, vibrant, and magical spirit whose perpetual smile brightened the lives of everyone she met. Born on February 17th, 1999, she embraced life with unconditional love and a heart filled with compassion. In her spare time, outside of school, Jordan dedicated herself to working with Sunday school children at our church and caring for our close family friend Brian Ward (Xan) Martin, affectionately known as Uncle Xan. She also adored spending time with, and caring for, her best friend, Emilee Beers.

Always a creative artist, Jordan had a passion for drawing, anime, cosplay, and all things Disney. Her colorful personality and gentle demeanor shone through in her artwork, whether in drawings, paintings, sculptures, or ceramics. She signed each piece with the name "Aqureil," a creative persona she developed from an online screen name. "Aqureil" embodied her artistic soul and imaginative spirit.

Our first born grew up to be the glue that held our family together. She was the best big sister in the world, often gathering her brothers, Spencer and Tyler, for bus trips to nearby shopping centers or simply to steal them away for a day of fun and comradere.

The impact Jordan had on her friends and family was profound. When asked about their favorite memories, her friends recalled the countless hours she spent in ceramics class, brainstorming and creating cute little clay creatures. Her memory lives on in the hearts of all who knew her. The church community remembers her as a bright and joyful presence, always making others laugh and smile. Her friends deeply feel her absence, fondly recalling Disney outings, youth events, and her welcoming nature that brought everyone together.

There is one specific element in this book that was inspired entirely by Jordan and added as a tribute. Her online username, “Aqureil,” has been woven into a significant mystical artifact called The Ring of Aqureil. This ring reflects Jordan’s artistic brilliance and represents her unique ability to bring people together. Just as Jordan was a unifying force in our lives, the ring plays a vital role in the story’s resolution, holding a crucial place in the story’s climax.

Jordan left a legacy of love, kindness, and creativity. Though her life was tragically cut short, it was filled with joy, laughter, and heartfelt connections.

Jordan Kaitlyn Block, your memory will forever be a blessing on our family and an inspiration to all who knew you. We love you endlessly and will carry you in our hearts until the end of time.

The Dragon Codex: Quest for the Relics of Design

Published by David Block
Tustin, California

Cover illustration by Abby Watson
Interior layout by David Block
Editing by Matthew Greenacre

ISBN: 9798218981563
Library of Congress Control Number: 2024913054

First Edition: September 2024
10 9 8 7 6 5 4 3 2 1

For information about bulk purchases or special sales, please contact:
David Block
Email: Magic@TheDragonCodexBK.com
Web: www.TheDragonCodexBK.com

Please share your thougths. Consider leaving a review on Amazon, Barnes & Noble, Goodreads, or your favorite bookseller.

Table of Contents

Prologue
Draconia: The Hidden Realm

Hidden from the outside world, the realm of Draconia thrived behind a veil of ancient magic. This powerful enchantment shielded the land from prying eyes, ensuring its wonders remained undisturbed.

At the heart of Draconia lay the capital city of Everbright, a bustling metropolis where dragons of all kinds gathered, their scales glinting under the vibrant city lights. For millennia, Everbright had stood as a hub of creativity and innovation, with every dragon contributing to the rich tapestry of Draconian culture. It was a place where dragons lived, worked, played, and relaxed, their lives intertwined in a celebration of design and artistry—unseen by the rest of the world.

Yet, despite its brilliance, Everbright was not without its secrets. Hidden relics of immense power, known only to a select few, held the key to Draconia's design heritage. These relics were the source of the city's creative energy, and their protection was vital. Like many magical realms, Draconia possessed its own ancient powers, accessible only through rituals long forgotten or now relegated to myth.

The dragons of Everbright lived day after day under the protection of Draconia's ancient magic, unaware of the adventures and mysteries looming ahead. Beneath the city's shining surface, whispers of forgotten legends stirred, hinting at deeper magic coursing through Draconia's veins. But the enchantments shielding their world would soon face trials like never before, testing the bonds of friendship and creativity. Only the bravest and most imaginative dragons could unlock these secrets, uncovering the true essence of their realm. The time for heroes was near, and soon, Draconia's hidden layers would reveal wonders—and dangers—no dragon could have imagined.

Chapter 1
The Three Relics

The final artifact was hers at last!

After years of investigating and searching, she had finally found the piece she had scoured every dark corner for. Thoughts of the relic had consumed her mind; every waking minute was spent trying to seize it, and now, it was hers at long last.

The weather outside seemed to agree with her, flashing lightning across the dark sky. It wanted to be part of the dark deeds unfolding, making its presence known.

To think the final artifact was right under her nose this whole time was almost comical. Celestia let out a slight cackle. She couldn't help herself as she made her way down the secret staircase. Her claws clinked on the stone floor and the coldness whipped at her scales.

Celestia was large even for a dragon. Her silver scales glinted in the little light from the cavern she was now in. Her dark eyes scanned the cavern through circular glasses with gold frames. For so long, she had yearned to place the last relic down here!

Sparks seemed to crackle in the air, even though the staircase was deep underground.

She had done it. The three Relics of Design were hers and she was not letting anyone else find or use them ever again. She was making sure of it.

Making her way through several caverns and rooms filled with unusual and strange artifacts that would make your head spin, Celestia rushed through it all, unblinking at her surroundings.

Even passing through different worlds didn't faze Celestia. After all, she had seen them many times before, most of them being her own creation.

Her mind was currently on one thing and one thing only—to hide the last relic where nobody else could ever get their claws on it.

Using all the skills and power she had gained; she sealed the relic with magic in a world nobody even knew existed. She felt a warmth inside her like she had never felt before—it was the feeling of success. Of contentment. Of wickedness.

The three legendary Relics of Design were all down here now, all for her. Nobody would be able to get through the brilliance of her designs. They couldn't make their way through her booby-trapped caverns, her genius puzzles and magic. Even if they could somehow get through it all, she still had her spiders. The spiders would get them. They always did.

First, she was able to find The Palette of Chromatia that was relatively easy to get hold of compared to the other relics. The Compass of Composition was tricky, she had to admit, as she used everything she had to bargain with Goblins to gain some information from them that helped her to discover where the Compass was located.

But the most difficult yet was the Quill of Typographus which was now finally hers! It had been years.

Three legendary relics were all hers, now hidden away forever.

Celestia grinned like a Cheshire cat returning to her office. She was back in the realm of Draconia, and not a soul knew what she had done.

Design and creativity would never be the same again in Draconia—a land filled with dragons, protected by ancient magic. Celestia was so pleased with herself as she settled down at her desk to make a start on dull paperwork.

A job well done, even if she said so herself.

She didn't even notice her assistant, Grocklepot, had been in her office this whole time, as he often was able to get around silently, unnoticed.

"Ahem," Grocklepot made a loud and annoying noise suddenly from the shadows.

Celestia had already been going through her papers and they

spilled out of her claws as Grocklepot made her jump. "Grocklepot! How many times do I need to tell you to make your presence known whenever you're in a room?"

"That's what I was doing, Ms. Celestia. I made sure to make a noise as soon as you had sat down at your desk, like you told me to." Grocklepot said slowly.

Ever since he started working for Celestia at Flametail Design, her colleagues didn't know what to do with Grocklepot. He was tiny and had a strange hump on his back. His scales were a mixture of ugly grays and greens, his fangs yellow and protruding. He was pretty much useless and weird. So strange to talk to, so unlike them, and eventually he had been dumped with Celestia as her assistant.

It had annoyed Celestia, but Grocklepot had come in useful at times and he was above all else, faithful to her. He would do whatever was required which was a rare skill these days.

"Yes, can you at least make yourself known once I am in the same room, please? What do you want from me anyway? I am very busy today." Celestia said, sighing as she picked up the papers from the floor.

"I am sorry, Ms. Celestia, I will be more careful from now on..." Grocklepot groveled.

"Yes, yes, yes. So, what is it? Spit it out Grocklepot."

Grocklepot shifted his weight uneasily. Celestia knew there was some sort of bad news he was keeping from her, and he didn't want to say.

"Well, you know how we've been working on the secret project, and now that you have all three legendary relics..." Grocklepot began, his voice shaky.

Celestia leapt to her feet and slammed her office door shut. "Hush, Grocklepot! Are you trying to broadcast our secret to the entire office? Now, what is it? What do you need to tell me?"

Grocklepot's eyes bulged as he shifted nervously. "Well, um... even though we have the three relics safely hidden—there's... there's something else."

Celestia's patience was wearing thin. "Yes, Grocklepot, I'm well aware we have the relics. What do you think I've been doing all this time? Now stop stalling and spit it out!" She began to absently toy with a crystal paperweight on her desk, a replica of herself from when she became CEO of Flametail Design.

Grocklepot took a deep breath. "I'm sorry, Ms. Celestia, but... there's a fourth relic," he blurted out, wincing as he instinctively ducked, as if bracing himself for a blow.

Celestia dropped the crystal paperweight. It shattered on the stone floor into a million pieces.

"Another relic?" Celestia could barely speak. Maybe she hadn't heard Grocklepot correctly.

He nodded silently. "There are three Relics of Design that the legendary designers were entrusted to protect. But there is also a hidden secret relic, meaning there are four relics in total and you only have three of them."

Celestia let out an almighty roar that shook the walls of the building and could be heard all across Draconia.

Chapter 2
The Black Cloak

"No."

"Nope."

"Not that."

"Not that, either."

Another balled-up piece of paper hit the wall beside Draco's desk as the green dragon hid his head in his paws. He'd never felt this stuck creatively before in his life. Summer vacation was supposed to be free time to make new things and interesting art that wasn't being restrained by guidelines or what his teachers thought he should be working on. He knew the concepts of art inside and out. So why did he suddenly feel stuck?

Draco let out a deep sigh, feeling the frustration clawing at him as he stared at the pile of crumpled papers scattered across his desk. His attempts at creating something new felt futile, and the weight of his creative block seemed heavier than ever. Just then, there was a soft knock on his door before it creaked open. His mother, Ryuna, stepped in, bending down to scoop up a few crumpled papers that had rolled onto the floor, her warm smile instantly bringing a sense of comfort to the room.

"You've been at this for hours, Little Flame," she said gently. "Sometimes, the best ideas come when you're not trying so hard to find them."

Draco looked up at her, managing a small smile. "I know, Mom, but I've felt like I can't do anything creative all day."

Ryuna crossed the room and placed a comforting hand on his shoulder. "It's okay to take a break. Step away for a moment, clear your mind. You might be surprised at what ideas can come when you least expect it."

Draco nodded, appreciating her words even if he wasn't sure they'd help right now. "Thanks, Mom."

She gave his shoulder a gentle squeeze before grabbing an armful of the crumpled papers and heading toward the door. “I’ll be downstairs if you need anything. And don’t worry too much—creativity has a way of finding you when the time is right.”

As his mom left the room, Draco took a deep breath, feeling a bit more at ease. He turned back to his desk, staring at the crumpled papers and scattered sketches. Despite his mother’s comforting words, the frustration still gnawed at him. He picked up his pencil again, determined to make something work, but the lines on the page just wouldn’t come together. He narrowed his eyes at the page, frustration tightening his grip on the pencil as his tail flicked restlessly behind him.

Moments later, Draco heard the familiar sound of the front door opening, followed by the excited chatter of Lumi and Arka. They let themselves in, as they often did, and made their way straight to his room. He didn’t even have time to dwell on his mother’s advice before his friends burst in, filling his room with their usual energy.

“Draco?” his best friend, Lumi, said, blinking at him as she stepped into the room. Pastel paint was smeared across her blue, scaly forearms, a sign that she’d been working on her own art project earlier. She took in the scene—Draco slumped over his desk, his tail flicking restlessly, and the scattered papers—and her expression softened. “Are you okay? You look really stressed out.”

Draco sighed, a small puff of steam escaping from between his fangs. “I’m fine, guys. I just don’t feel like I’m getting anywhere with this project,” he muttered under his breath; his frustration evident in his tone.

Arka, his other best friend, hung from the pipes on the ceiling, noticing the tension in Draco’s posture. “It’s no wonder you’re stressed,” she said, her tone more analytical. “You’ve been at this for hours, haven’t you? Sometimes, a break really does help.”

“When I’m stressed out, I like to eat a snack,” offered Lumi, holding out a cookie to Draco.

“Where did you get that from?” Arka asked, now upside down, peering curiously at the cookie.

Lumi leaned in close, glancing around as if sharing a great secret, and almost whispered with a grin, "Pocket cookie."

Draco sighed again, this time with a hint of amusement as he took the cookie from Lumi and crunched into it. "Thanks, Lumi," he said, a bit of the tension easing from his shoulders.

Lumi picked up one of his balled-up papers from the floor. She uncrumpled it and held it up to the light, revealing some mint green and bubblegum pink claw marks as she turned it in circles. "This is so pretty! Um..." Lumi paused, momentarily enchanted by the beauty. Draco took it from her and turned it the other way around. "Oh, I see!" Lumi said, raising an eyebrow as understanding dawned on her.

"Hmmf. I don't see," said Arka. She held onto the pipe with one set of her metal-adorned paws and hung down, flaring her wings to stabilize. The posters and drawings on Draco's basement bedroom walls fluttered a bit. She took the crumpled sheet of paper from Lumi and inspected it. "I believe it is supposed to be a map of Draconia. However, the proportions are... well, how can I say this... a hot mess," Arka stated.

"Arka!" Lumi exclaimed, swiping at Arka with her tail. "That's not very nice," she scolded.

"She's right, though," Draco said miserably, pushing cookie crumbs off his desk. "I just wanted to make something super cool for the design contest, but I don't really know anything about making maps."

Oh, you mean the giant, super-prestigious design contest that Mentor Blaze couldn't stop talking about at last week's assembly? The one where he practically breathed fire from excitement?" Lumi quipped with a grin.

"That's it," Draco said, kicking at one of the scrunched-up maps.

"What's the prize for that contest again?" Lumi asked, eyes sparking with interest.

"A horde of treasure, directly from the largest design firm in Draconia," Arka said, importantly. "It's rare that the Design Council plans something like this. I don't believe they've ever partnered with a business, either. It's strange. I have been following it closely. However, maps are not my area of expertise either." She dropped to the floor with a whoosh and a thump.

"Ooh!" exclaimed Lumi, almost throwing her paintbrush at the excitement of the idea that had just entered her head. "We could totally go to the library and see if they have any books on mapmaking!"

"That sounds boring," Draco said. "Who wants to read a book about art? Why not just make it instead?" he asked.

"You are incorrect. Books are the greatest thing in the world!" Arka said.

"I only like the ones with pictures," Lumi said. "But I bet we could find mapmaking books with pictures! I mean, maps basically are just fancy pictures, right?" she said with a mischievous grin, her eyes sparkling with excitement.

Draco considered this and said, "I could definitely use a break from this room."

"Me too," Arka said. "I mean, do you know how many cobwebs are up here? I've nearly inhaled approximately five spiders," Arka exclaimed, waving her paws around to clear the invisible webs.

"Ew," Lumi said. With a determined nod, she said again, "We really do need to get out of here. It's almost night, and we've barely done anything all day. This is so *not* what summer is all about!"

"Exactly why we should do something entertaining, such as going to the library," Arka offered.

Draco hesitated, his eyes stopping on the scattered papers one last time. But Lumi and Arka's energy was contagious and he felt the tight knot of frustration slowly loosen. Maybe a break wouldn't be so bad after all.

Draco nodded decisively, grateful for the break from tying his brain in knots. "If you say so," he remarked. His tone was tinged with a hint of amusement.

The three friends cleared up Draco's workspace and headed

downstairs. The clock over the fireplace told the friends they needed to hurry to the library before it closed.

The library was next to their school, Draconia Middle, and only a few minutes' walk from Draco's cheerful little house that he shared with his mom and dad. It was close to sunset, and a slight breeze ruffled through the full, leafy trees lining the path. Draco thought it was nice outside. Lumi complained that she was too hot, which was probably because she had been running in circles around Draco and Arka as they walked.

The Draconian Library, other than the esteemed Council Hall, was the crown jewel of Draconia. It was so tall that the shadow it cast darkened the path nearly a full minute before the friends got to the front doors.

"We should hurry," Arka called from the doorway. Her mouth was curled up slightly in a tiny, crooked-fang smile. "It closes in just over an hour," she emphasized.

Before the friends had a chance to speak, a whooshing noise came from above, and something landed in front of them, large wings folding slowly beneath a black cloak. A dark hood covered the figure's face, obscuring their identity.

"Hey, could you please let us through? We need to get inside!" Lumi said.

The figure didn't move or say anything except to hold out a paw, with a note inside.

Arka moved forward and took the note.

The figure flew off immediately without saying anything.

"Hmm, they seemed nice." Lumi said.

"What does it say?" Draco moved close to Arka to peer over her shoulder.

"It's sealed from somewhere called The Midnight Shadows..." Arka said. She opened the seal with a claw and read aloud:

DO NOT TRUST CELESTIA.

WE WILL BE WATCHING.

Chapter 3
The Secret Passageway

"Huh?" Lumi breathed.

"Who will be watching?" Arka said and turned the note over but found nothing else.

Draco wasn't sure who it was or what they meant, but he felt like he had to trust what they were saying. Like it was a warning or something that he should heed.

"I have no idea. Let's go inside before it closes," Draco said leading the way through the library.

Draco had often gone into the library for school projects, but he could never get used to it. Floor-to-ceiling windows lined the walls, providing lots of natural light for reading and studying. Several students—mostly Draco's age or older—sat at desks, tails curled around paws or dusting the floor with excitement, reading, noting, or studiously typing on computers.

Lumi floated above them, picking dried paint off her arms, uninterested in anything except exactly what they came for, while Arka skittered through the stacks, her paws plucking books from shelves and looping back to discard them after a quick scan, occasionally offering up a fun fact.

Arka asked, "Were you aware that dragons' lungs have evolved over in Havenfall to hold more steam units because of the dry atmosphere? Did you know it's a mystery who designed the first Draconian map? Those delicious apples native to the tropics supposedly went extinct before Everbright University scientists could return them. Isn't that just the..."

"Arka, hold on," Draco said. Arka halted in her path, and Lumi landed precariously on a shelf of books about the history of farming. "What was that second thing you just said? Was it about the map of Draconia?"

Arka had been about to discard the book, but instead, she turned and offered it to Draco. "According to this, not a single dragon knows who designed the first map of Draconia. Fascinating, isn't it?"

Draco read the title aloud. "The Codex of Design." It was green and leathery, sort of like Draco himself, and the writing was gold—but the author's name had been clawed out. As Draco looked closer to try and figure out some of the letters, he noticed that "Draconia" had been embossed in the same gold lettering right under the title, next to a small brick shape with an arrow pointing to it. It looked like handwriting, yet it was embedded in the front of the book, just like the title. "That's interesting," Draco mused. He tucked the book into his bag, resolving to read it after they had found more books. "Let's see the design section."

The library was like a maze, and the closer Draco and his friends got to the back of the building, the more disorganized the stacks became. When they got to the design section, dusty and in disarray, the wall behind it was made of bricks, which was a strange contrast to the rest of the building. Painted onto the bricks was a faded map mural of Everbright, the city they lived in.

Arka ran one claw along the bricks with a screeching noise. "Interesting design choice," she remarked, her curiosity piqued.

"Especially for the design section," Lumi piped up. "I mean, you'd think they'd know better. I like the painting, though! The colors are nice."

Draco was too busy looking through the books on the shelf to pay attention to them. There weren't many books on design. He saw a few about flags and drawing compositions, but nothing specifically jumped out at him about maps.

"Why would a dragon be writing about maps?" He mumbled to himself under his breath in frustration. Remembering the book in his bag that Arka had found earlier and thinking it might be his only hope, he pulled it out and opened it. The introduction was a concise page that read:

Design is a highly praised art in the land of Draconia. However, no one knows where this fine art originated regarding the intricate design of the city's maps. There are records of a Mapmaker Chief on the first Draconian Council, but no record indicates this dragon's name.

Who was the original Mapmaker Chief of Draconia, the one who designed the first full map of the entire realm? Did they write themselves out of the history books, or did someone else strike them from the record? And if so, why?

"Weird," Draco murmured.

To his surprise, when he turned the page to continue reading, it was blank! It continued the next and the one after that, too. In fact, other than the introduction, the whole book was empty.

He closed the book and stared at it. "Arka, Lumi, come look," he called, and his two friends drifted over. "Arka, did you see that there's nothing else in here?" he asked.

"I only read the introduction," Arka admitted, taking the book from Draco's claws and flipping through it, confirming it was indeed blank.

"The introduction was all there was to read!" Draco said. "Something bizarre is going on here. And did you see the cover?"

"Yes. No author, and 'Draconia' written in gold leaf," Arka rattled off.

"Well, there was an author, but the name has been scratched out. See? Someone really didn't want us to know who wrote this book," Draco affirmed.

"Maybe the author was rebelling because the bricks are ugly," Lumi piped up jokingly. Arka and Draco both looked at her in confusion. "What? What did I say exactly?"

"What possibly gave you the idea the book had something to do with the brick wall?" Arka asked. "We didn't find this book in the design section," she added, her tone tinged with skepticism.

"It was just a joke. I mean..." Lumi tapped a claw on the cover, where the brick shape was etched. "Isn't this a brick?" She pointed at the wall. "And it says Draconia, and there's a map on the wall...? Hmm, my theory's kinda falling apart now. Maybe I'm reaching. It was just supposed to be a joke, after all," she concluded nervously, hoping to diffuse any tension her speculation may have caused.

"Wait a moment." Arka skittered over to the wall and began to search. “Lumi, you might be a genius.”

“Thanks!” Lumi chirped. “What did I do?”

Arka smirked. “Oh, just being the light in my day, as always!”

Draco followed after Arka. “What are you looking for Arka?”

She pointed at the cover. “Lumi was correct. The brick was an interesting design choice. It also struck me as much more modern than the rest of the walls. Ergo, someone built this wall later than the rest of the library,” she concluded, admiring Lumi’s insightful observation.

Draco’s brow furrowed. “So, you think… that same someone was trying to hide something?”

“Perhaps the same dragon who hid the author’s name. It’s simply a hunch. However…” Arka pointed at the brick on which the artist had painted the star, indicating where Draconia was. If Draco looked closely, he could see a seam around the brick where the paint had cracked, like that one particular brick had been moved before.

“I think your hunch was right,” Draco said in wonder.

“Dang!” Lumi exclaimed. “I need to make jokes more often!” Before Draco or Arka could protest, she hopped over and pressed the brick with a paint-stained paw.

“Lumi!” Arka and Draco both yelped at once. Draco tensed in fear. He didn’t know if the brick would do anything or if the idea was even right, but he had expected to have at least a second to think about it before they tried anything.

The three dragonlets watched in wonder and anxiety as the brick impressed into the wall like a neat click of a button, and suddenly, the entire brick wall began to fold. Brick after brick spun in on itself, creating a new passageway in the middle of the design section.

“Magic!” Lumi breathed.

“Technology,” Arka corrected.

The draft emanating from the new doorway chilled Draco, and he shivered. It was too pitch black to see anything beyond the first few steps into the cavernous tunnel, which was only about as tall as a fully grown dragon and half as wide.

“Should we... go inside?” Draco asked. “We just magicked a hole in the library wall. I think we have to go in now,” he added.

“We have no supplies, no dragon knows our location, and it’s easily the most frightening place I’ve ever laid eyes on,” Arka listed, pacing back and forth in front of the passageway.

Draco took a cautious step inward, then one more. The cold air felt like it was beckoning him in, whispering secrets in his ears.

“I think we have to go in,” Draco said. And it really felt like he had to. It was like it was calling him and his friends towards something.

The book he found had a strange energy; he could feel some sort of ancient magic emanating from it. He couldn’t explain it, but it was like he was in the right place at the right time. This was the first time he had really felt purpose in his little life in his little town, and he wasn’t going to ignore it for some silly reason like being afraid.

Chapter 4
The Guardian

Lumi pushed past Draco, bounding a few steps forward into the cavernous darkness. "You don't have to tell me twice!" she exclaimed.

"This is a bad idea," Arka said, eyes wide. "It is really a terrible idea. We should get help. Find adult dragons who know better about this place than us."

Draco turned back to her. "It's okay if you're scared. Do you want to keep watch?"

Arka bristled. "I am not frightened."

Lumi cocked her head. "But you said—"

"I simply said that the tunnel looks frightening. I did not say I was frightened," Arka asserted, her voice steady despite the ominous surroundings.

"What's the difference?" Lumi asked, confused.

Arka clarified, "Well, one describes the thing itself, and the other describes how a dragon feels, which is not to say that's how I feel, in particular."

"Guys," Draco interrupted. "Are we going or not?" His voice cut through Arka and Lumi's indecisive murmurs with a sense of urgency.

Arka sighed. "Note that I am extremely not on board with this. But I'm not letting you two get into danger without some brain power to help you." She stepped into the passageway with the two of them.

Lumi clapped in excitement. "Yay! Adventure!

Arka shook her head, clearly still worried, and Draco led his friends into the tunnel.

The moment Arka's tail passed the threshold, there was a deep rumbling from underneath the ground, and the bricks began to swing and twist around again. Lumi let out a yelp and tried to run back out into the design section, but the last brick filled in the instant before she got to it, and she banged her snout into the wall. "Oof!"

Draco and his friends were in darkness. Determined to help, Lumi stepped forward, her gaze focused on the pitch-black surroundings. She took a deep breath, summoning her magical flame. She could feel the energy coursing through her, but it still took all of her concentration to bring it to life.

"Hang on," Draco said as he fumbled for his bag, pulling out his new notebook and rolling it between his paws. He held it up toward Lumi. "Can you light this? Just aim your flame carefully."

Lumi hesitated for a moment but then squared her shoulders. She took another breath, feeling the familiar warmth building inside her, and released a controlled stream of blue flame in Draco's direction. The light flickered against the darkness as she carefully aimed for the notebook, trying her best to keep her control steady.

The blue flames danced across the pages, crackling softly as they took hold. Lumi's focus was unwavering, and for a few moments, she managed to sustain the flame long enough to ignite the notebook. As the fire grew brighter, the blue flames began to shift, turning into a glowing golden hue.

"Whoa," Draco said, watching the transformation. Now holding a makeshift torch, he grinned. The hall was dimly lit, and Lumi beamed with pride, having successfully controlled her flame, even if just for a short while. Lumi blinked a few times as the golden light illuminated the tunnel. She glanced at the torch, then back at Draco with a smirk. "Well, at least I didn't set your horns on fire this time," she quipped, clearly pleased with herself. "Guess who just graduated from 'tiny sparks' to 'full-blown torch'? That's right, lil' old me!"

Arka puffed steam, not amused in the slightest. "Now that you've gotten us stuck here, I think we should formulate a plan instead of continuing on with no possible way of knowing what awaits us."

Draco gestured down the hall. "Look on the bright side! At least there's only one direction to go now."

"There's never only one solution. We could always try to open the door again," Lumi stated.

Draco held the torch up to the wall, and Lumi tapped the bricks. "It's just a wall from this side, I think," she said.

"Well," Draco said. He turned back towards the dark unknown, the end of the hall seeming too far away for the golden torchlight to touch. It still beckoned to him, filling him with the urge to explore. "I'm going this way, and Arka can keep watch."

"There's no possible way I'm letting you two go down there alone," Arka insisted, ever protective of her two best friends.

Golden torchlight illuminated stone brick walls, intricately carved with a language that Draco couldn't read and had never seen before. As Draco and his friends got only a little further down, sconces shaped like dragon heads lit up, orbs of blue fire in their jaws. Lumi stared at one in wonder, almost scorching her nose on it when she got too close. Draco tossed down the flaming notebook just as it began to flicker out. Suddenly, the flames licked up from its edges and the entire book was consumed in seconds, disintegrating into a small pile of ash that settled on the stone floor.

The ceiling above him arched low, barely higher than the doorway. Unlike the ornate, gilded designs of the library outside, this space was smooth and gray—simple but elegant in its own way. Even if Draco felt uneasy in the unfamiliar surroundings, he couldn't help but appreciate the contrast in styles. After all, he was an artist at heart.

"This hall looks different from the library," Draco said. "Do you think the people who built the library know the passageway exists?" Draco's question lingered in the air, mingling with the faint scent of old parchment. Lumi pondered for a moment before replying.

"I'm certain they do. How else would it have appeared?" Lumi's eyes sparkled with excitement as she listened to Draco's words.

"True, but it looks like the janitors have never set claw in here," Draco said.

Lumi batted away a cobweb irritably. "Gosh, and it sure smells like it."

Draco took a sniff. Indeed, it smelled damp and mildewy, like someone had left a wet towel on the floor somewhere—or ten wet towels.

They continued their descent down the hall, the angle growing steeper with every step, their eyes scanning the walls for any sign of change. But the passage remained eerily uniform, with the same strange carvings and unsettling dragon heads lighting their way, flickering into existence every few paces. Lumi insisted they'd been walking for "a super long time," though Arka, ever practical, assured her it had only been about five minutes.

At last, the passageway opened up into a grand arched gateway, looming ahead like a portal to another world. The entrance was flanked by two towering statues, their faces cold and indifferent, as if they had guarded this threshold for centuries without a single flicker of emotion. These sentinels didn't welcome visitors; they stood as silent warnings to those who dared to pass.

"That's not ominous at all," Arka muttered, still displeased about being outvoted.

The hallway opened into a cavern that looked like it had been carved directly into the bedrock under the library. The floor was rough and slippery, water trickling down the walls and collecting in puddles.

"I've never been in a cave before!" squealed Lumi, her excited voice bouncing off the walls in a loud echo. But unlike a normal echo, this one didn't go away—it started getting louder until all three dragons had to clap their paws over their ears.

"What is that?" Draco yelled over the din.

Lumi's excitable shriek slowly morphed into a booming voice, as loud and sharp as a clap of thunder. "GREETINGS, DRAGONLETS," the voice roared, reverberating through the cavern with an echo that layered multiple high and low voices together. Despite the mix, the voice had a distinctly feminine quality, deep and resonant, that sent shivers down their spines.

Draco swung his head around frantically, trying to see where the giant voice was coming from. "Who are you? What is this place?" he yelled out.

"YOU HAVE BEEN CHOSEN," the voice replied, leaving Draco's questions unanswered. "STEP FORWARD. YOU HAVE NOTHING TO FEAR." Draco, Arka, and Lumi all backed against each other in the center of the round chamber, forming a three-pointed star of fearful friends. "THAT'S CLOSE ENOUGH, YOUNG ONES," she said, the warmth in her tone contrasting with the power of her earlier words.

The Guardian's voice filled the cavern, strong and steady, but something about it stirred an uneasy familiarity in Draco. As he listened, the light in the chamber shifted, casting sharp shadows that seemed to form purposeful patterns along the stone walls. The shapes were clean and precise, almost like designs carved with intent. Draco felt an odd pull toward them, as if the Guardian was trying to communicate more than just words—like there was a message hidden in the way the space itself was arranged, waiting for him to discover it.

"Um, excuse me, sorry," Lumi piped up. "But why are we here?"

"I AM THE GUARDIAN OF DESIGN." As the Guardian's words echoed through the chamber, the blue flames in the sconces flared brighter, casting light all across the stone walls. Lumi yelped in surprise and instinctively leaned closer to Arka as the room filled with an intense, eerie blue glow.

"AND I AM IN DIRE NEED OF YOUR HELP."

"You need our help?" Draco asked, looking back up toward the vaulted ceiling of the cave. "But... we're just kids." His voice quivered with uncertainty.

"AGE IS NO MEASURE OF GREATNESS. YOU THREE HAVE A DEEP WELL OF POTENTIAL WAITING TO BE UNLOCKED," the Guardian of Design said.

Draco took a deep breath, trying to steady himself. He looked around at his friends, drawing strength from their presence. "I... I guess you're right," he said, determination slowly replacing his uncertainty.

"What is the problem?" Arka cut in. She was all business as usual, even though her pupils were dilated in fear when Draco looked over at her. Lumi was stuck to her side, arms wrapped tightly around Arka's middle. Draco reached back with the paw not holding the book and placed what he hoped was a comforting paw on Lumi's paint-splattered shoulder.

THREE OF THE LEGENDARY RELICS OF DESIGN, MAGICAL KEYS TO DRACONIA'S SAFETY AND SECRECY, HAVE BEEN STOLEN. THESE ARTIFACTS, CRUCIAL FOR MAINTAINING THE REALM'S CONCEALMENT FROM THE OUTSIDE WORLD AND NURTURING ITS RICH CULTURE OF ART, DESIGN, AND CREATIVITY, HAVE VANISHED.

NOW, THE THEFT OF A FOURTH, SECRET RELIC THREATENS TO UNRAVEL THE VERY FABRIC OF OUR KINGDOM. WITHOUT THESE RELICS, DRACONIA'S MAGIC WEAKENS, EXPOSING US TO UNKNOWN DANGERS AND ERODING THE CREATIVE SPIRIT THAT HAS LONG SUSTAINED US. AN ANCIENT MAGICAL RITUAL, NOW FORGOTTEN, ONCE RAN DEEP THROUGH THE VEINS OF DRACONIA, AND ITS LOST POWER NOW JEOPARDIZES OUR VERY EXISTENCE.

"Stolen?" Draco asked, looking down at the book he was holding.

"THE AUTHOR OF THIS BOOK HAS BEEN STRICKEN, NOT JUST FROM THE COVER... BUT FROM OUR HISTORY, FOREVER BANISHED."

Above where the three dragonlets were standing, an eerie, see-through image appeared of the same book Draco was holding. The book's hologram opened, the blank pages flipping as if caught in a strong wind. "THE FIRST MAPMAKER OF DRACONIA, ALONG WITH OTHER MIGHTY DRAGONS, HAVE FALLEN UNDER THIS DARK SHADOW. THEIR ASTOUNDING ACCOMPLISHMENTS REMAIN, BUT THEIR RELICS ARE VANISHING. A POWER GREATER THAN MINE IS STEALING THEM AWAY."

"Greater than yours?" Lumi questioned. "But... your voice is like thunder, and you make books come to life!"

"I AM MORTAL," the Guardian boomed. "WE ARE NOT FULLY CERTAIN WHO THIS BEING IS OR WHAT THEY CAN DO, BUT YOU HAVE THE TOOLS TO STOP THEM. YOU MUST FIND THE FOUR RELICS AND RETURN THEM TO RESTORE DESIGN TO DRACONIA. THE KEY TO THIS LIES IN THE ANCIENT RITUAL."

Lumi's wings drooped as the weight of the revelation sank in. "This is terrible! Our whole world depends on these relics. We need to find them and bring them back. Draconia's magic and creativity are at stake!"

Chapter 5
The Closing Walls

"Okay," Draco said. The way he saw it, he hadn't really found his purpose in life yet. He was just a dragonlet. But he felt, for some reason, like he was meant to come here. Something greater than himself had guided him to this place. Maybe it was the need to create, maybe his destiny, but it was something out there that thought he could make a difference, or perhaps even save his home. "Okay," he said again, feeling the power of the book he had found. "I'm in."

"Me too," Lumi piped up, looking towards the ceiling. She stood up straight, letting go of Arka. She still seemed a little scared, but Draco could read the determination on her face. "This is the kind of adventure that great stories are written about! There's no way we can walk away from this mystery, right?" She turned to Draco with a hopeful look. "Right, Draco?"

Draco nodded in agreement.

"This is going to end badly," Arka said as if she'd done the mental calculations already and come up with a surefire answer. She cocked her head, curiosity getting the better of her. "If I help, will you show me how you've created this holographic book?" The image of the book morphed into a silent thumbs-up. "Well, then. It can't hurt to try."

"DRACONIA WILL REVERE YOU, DRAGONLETS," the Guardian said a note of pride in their thunderous voice.

"Cool," Draco said intelligently.

Lumi tried to bow to the Guardian and almost fell flat on her snout.

"So, these heroes will save the creative world," muttered Arka.

"IT SEEMS THAT WAY."

"What do we do?" Draco asked.

"THE CODEX OF DESIGN WILL GUIDE YOU," the Guardian

said simply.

"But there's nothing inside of it?" Lumi said in confusion.

Draco opened the book to its first blank page. To his astonishment, the page came alive with magic, bright shapes, and words materializing on the rough parchment as if guided by an unseen hand. It was Draconia, clearly, but not any Draconia that Draco knew—it was the perfect example of a map, and the color composition felt like it was shouting at him in the best way possible. Still, the places were all out of order.

Arka and Lumi peered over Draco's shoulder. "Wow," Lumi breathed.

"It's beautiful," Arka said with reverence. "The proportions? The lines? Impeccable. This is a map. Even with the locations mixed up like this."

"THIS CLUE IS ALL WE HAVE FOR THE FIRST DRACONIAN MAPMAKER. IT IS A PUZZLE THAT I'M CERTAIN YOU WILL BE ABLE TO SOLVE."

"At least we don't have school for another few weeks," Draco sighed, overwhelmed.

"BUT TO MAKE CERTAIN YOU ARE THE RIGHT DRAGON FOR THE JOB, YOU MUST SOLVE THE FIRST TEST OF PROWESS."

"Sounds great!" Lumi said. "What's prowess?" she asked.

"IT MEANS SKILL. CAPABILITY. IMAGINATION. PERSEVERANCE. ALL OF THESE ARE THE MARK OF A GREAT GRAPHIC DESIGNER." The hologram blinked out with a shower of sparkles and then reappeared—instead of a book, now the picture showed a collection of assorted, random blue lines, some straight, some angles, and some squiggling like worms. "FIND THE PASSWORD, FIVE CHARACTERS LONG, AND THE EXIT WILL SHOW WHERE YOU BELONG. IF YOU'RE STUCK AND THE WAY SEEMS BLIND, CHANGE YOUR PERSPECTIVE, AND THE ANSWER YOU'LL FIND. GOOD LUCK DRAGONLETS, MAY YOU BE STRONG."

"Wait!" cried Draco. "What's the password? How do we find it?" the Guardian didn't speak back to him, and the only noise in the chamber was the echo of his own words and the slow trickle of water down the walls.

"Maybe the lines form a map?" Arka wondered. "Such as the one in the book?" she suggested, her eyes alight with curiosity and hope.

"That doesn't make any sense," Draco said, looking down at the brightly colored map that had appeared moments before. "The colors don't match, and neither do any of the shapes." Lumi started walking in circles around the hologram as Draco and Arka discussed, seemingly just to have something to do.

"Could it be a language?" Draco offered. "Something we're supposed to try to translate?" His inquiry lingered, injecting a sense of intrigue into the conversation, leaving everyone pondering the mystery before them.

"But these lines don't spell anything out or form any kind of recognizable symbol," Arka said, her frustration evident.

Lumi hesitated, then tilted her head. "Um, actually... they do. Can't you see it?" Draco and Arka exchanged puzzled glances.

"What are you talking about, Lumi? They just look like random lines to me," Arka replied, still confused.

Lumi shook her head vigorously. "Nuh-uh! It's totally the letter S," she countered, her voice laced with playful certainty, daring Draco and Arka to challenge her assertion.

Draco trotted over to her and leaned down slightly so they were the same height. Sure enough, the lines in the middle combined made a scripted letter S. "She's right, Arka."

Arka ran to them. "What an interesting way of designing these letters!" She then stepped a few paces to the left, tilting her head. "From here, I see an H." Her observation added another layer to the mystery, fueling their determination to unravel its secrets.

"There's more?" Draco asked in wonder.

Lumi bounded just a few paces down, going up on her hind legs. "I see an E over here!"

Draco moved to the other side of the hologram, staring hard at the lines. Nothing made sense until the Guardian's words echoed in his mind, "*TRY CHANGING YOUR PERSPECTIVE.*" He crouched low, almost touching the floor. Slowly, the lines converged into something familiar. His eyes widened. "I see it... It's an R!" he said, excitement bubbling up inside him.

The dragonlets came together in the center of the chamber, bathed in the kaleidoscopic glow of the hologram. Arka tilted her head, studying the interplay of colors and shapes. "The fifth letter has to be here somewhere," she muttered.

Lumi fluttered her wings and pointed to a cluster of reflections on the cave ceiling. "Look! Up there, the lines are forming something."

Draco squinted and saw it too. "It looks like the letter C!" he exclaimed.

As they all watched, the blurry glow shimmered and solidified into lines, forming the letter C. "The Guardian said there are five characters in the password, so the C is the last one," Draco said.

"Ok," Arka said. "what words can be made with these five letters?"

"SHREC?" Lumi asked the ceiling hopefully.

Complete silence filled the chamber. Draco could swear even the water stopped trickling down the walls. Then, a grinding noise rattled its way to life, and the walls started moving, trickles of dust and particles billowing out where the water was just coming from. The stone edges of the cave were closing in on them like it was about to smash them flat!

"Is this supposed to happen?" Lumi squeaked.

"I don't believe so!" Arka yelled.

The stone walls ground closer and closer to them, inch by inch.

"Try a different combination of letters!" Draco cried out. He put his paws on the wall and tried to shove, hoping whatever was driving the walls could stop, but it pushed him along with the wall as if he wasn't doing anything.

"RESCH?" Lumi asked, directing her voice to the ceiling. The walls froze as if contemplating her answer. Draco exhaled deeply as he started to rest against the cold stone. But before they could even process it, the walls resumed their motion at a terrifyingly faster pace.

"Another word! Another word!" Arka yelled from the other wall. She was trying to push, too, and had about as much luck as Draco.

"I don't know!" Draco squeezed his eyes shut, frustration evident in his voice. "What about... SCHER?"

A low rumble shook the surrounding earth, louder than the moving walls. Lumi shrieked and jumped into Arka's arms, and Draco backed against them, certain the cave was about to crush them. Instead, the ground beneath their feet rumbled as if responding to an ancient command. As the three dragonlets watched, the wall ahead began to disassemble, each brick moving independently as though guided by an invisible hand. Light began to filter through the gaps, and the cool, musty air of the library drifted towards them. The bricks formed an archway, revealing the familiar sight of the library beyond.

"GO IN CREATIVITY, DRAGONLETS," the Guardian said. "NOTE WHAT YOU HAVE LEARNED IN THE BOOK. AND LET THE DESIGNERS OF THE PAST GUIDE YOUR CLAWS. FIND THE FOUR RELICS, DISCOVER THE ANCIENT RITUAL, BEFORE IT'S TOO LATE."

Arka set down Lumi and breathed a deep sigh of relief, smoke pouring from her jaws. "We did it." She sounded like she was trying to convince herself.

"I can't believe Draco squishing his face on the floor solved it!" Lumi said with a giggle. "And I can't believe the library almost turned us into a stack of dragon pancakes."

"Is that funny to you?" Arka asked her.

"Well, yeah, a little bit, now that it's not actually going to happen," Lumi admitted.

"We saved ourselves. And all it took was trying new answers when we failed and looking at it differently," Draco said. He took a pen from his bag and wrote in the map's margins: if stuck, try a change in perspective. Then, underneath, the mysterious password: SCHER.

"Often, the only way I can complete a project is to change how I look at it," Arka admitted. "It could be either by simply moving my head, in a physical sense, or just by telling myself to change how I feel about it. It works wonders."

"That's good advice, then," Draco said with a determined nod. "Come on, let's get out of here."

They could see the rows of bookshelves stretching into the distance and hear the soft whispers of the librarian letting dragons know that the library would close in five minutes. With renewed resolve, the three dragonlets walked through the magical archway and down the book-lined aisle from where they came. Before they could turn to look, the bricks that formed the archway had reshaped themselves into the blank wall, but it happened so quickly that they could only see the last brick sliding into place at the last instant.

"What... shall we do?" Arka asked, breaking the silence as they reached the door.

"I guess the first thing is to figure out what this word means." Draco pointed at the magic book, again indicating the word in the margins. SCHER. The three of them joined the steady stream of dragons leaving the library.

"No, the first thing is to go to bed!" Lumi yawned, waving at a dragon she seemed to know. "It's late!"

Draco sighed. His friend was right—he was beginning to feel the ache of tiredness under his scales. They had already had a long day, struggling with creative projects and solving puzzles that almost crushed them—even heroes needed to sleep sometimes.

"We should all get some rest," Arka agreed. She was tinkering with something mindlessly between two of her paws. "I may not be able to sleep tonight after that."

"Let's meet next to the Big Tree tomorrow," Draco decided. "We can go into the city and see if anyone has heard of this weird word."

Lumi nodded in agreement and put her paw in the center. "Team cheer!"

Arka sighed and put one of her free paws in the middle. Draco put his paw over theirs, and on the count of three, they all threw them in the air.

"Goooo, team!" Lumi cheered.

Chapter 6
Flametail Design

Draco spent a few hours before bed drawing maps aimlessly, and thoughts clouded with what he had learned that day. He made maps upside down, from the side, by folding the paper—all different ways. When he eventually got to bed, he felt like he barely blinked before it was morning again, and it was time for him to go meet his friends at the Big Tree in front of their school.

Draco, his small satchel slung across his shoulder, went down to the kitchen. His green scales glinted in the morning light as he took a piece of bread from the bread box and seared it with a jet of fire. The familiar tunes on the living room radio played softly in the background, filling the air with the last notes of an easy listening song his mother enjoyed. As he ate his toast, the song ended, and the voice of the news anchor took over—calm, yet colored with a touch of bewilderment.

"... Strange occurrences continue as the once-vibrant murals of Everbright begin to dull and fade away. Graphic designers report their works spontaneously erasing, leaving only faint outlines behind. Authorities are urging calm, though they admit they have no explanation for the loss of creativity. More at 11:00."

Draco frowned slightly as he listened to the newscast. It seemed like the all of Draconia was feeling off lately. Shaking the thought away, he glanced down at a note sitting on the dining table, catching his eye.

Hey, Little Flame, my projects are piling up, so I won't be around much this week. You can always find me at the office or ask the neighbors for anything. And, hey, if you're looking for a way to pass the time, we might have some work for you and your friends to do down here at the firm. Keep your fire burning bright! Love, Dad.

Draco carefully tucked the note from his father into his satchel, a soft smile crossing his face. His dad was always encouraging him to embrace the spark of creativity that ran in their family.

"Your mother thinks I'm too hard on you with all this design talk," he had once said with a laugh. "But she knows, just like I do, that you've got the heart of a true designer." That balance—his father's relentless passion for design and his mom's nurturing care—was what made their home such a special place to grow up.

Draco missed his dad but also liked having the house to himself for his projects. His neighbors were nice, and his mom made him food when needed.

Draco slung his satchel over his shoulder, ready to head out when his mother appeared in the doorway of the kitchen, wiping her hands on a dish towel.

"Off to meet Lumi and Arka?" she asked, her voice warm as the morning sun.

"Yeah," Draco nodded, still thinking about the note from his father.

Ryuna smiled, noticing the slight furrow in his brow. "Your father's always pushed himself to work hard, but remember, it's just as important to find time for yourself, Little Flame. Balance is key."

Draco giggled softly, feeling a little less worried. "I will, Mom. Thanks. See you later."

"Be safe," Ryuna called after him as he stepped out into the bright morning.

Once outside, Draco stopped for a moment, tucking the note carefully into his bag along with the magic book and a few snacks for later. The morning air was crisp, and the walk to the Big Tree was a welcome chance to clear his head. The Big Tree, a giant oak that towered over the front yard of Draconia Middle, was a familiar and comforting sight. During the school year, it was a popular spot where kids would gather to eat lunch or play games, but in the quiet of summer, it stood serene and empty.

When Draco arrived, he spotted his friends already waiting for him. Lumi was lost in her sketchbook, doodling intently, while Arka was busy tinkering with the small contraption she'd been building the previous night.

“You’re late!” Lumi chided.

“Ignore her,” Arka said, without bothering to look up from her gadget-making. “She got here only a minute or two before you arrived.” Her words carried a note of reassurance.

“...ready to go to the city?” Draco asked. “Maybe while we’re there, we can visit my dad.” He thought for a second of the note, probably getting crinkled in his satchel.

“I haven’t seen him in quite some time.” Arka said, putting the gadget she had been working on into one of the bags on her tool belt. “I suppose we could ask around at his place of business. Where does he work again?”

“Ooh, ooh!” Lumi dropped her pen to raise her paw. “I know this one! He’s a designer, right?” Her excitement bubbled over, injecting a moment of levity into their midst as they delved deeper into their discussion.

“Yeah, he works for Flametail Design in Downtown,” Draco said.

“I bet graphic designers would know a lot about other famous designers, right? What if they could help us determine why their names are going poof?” Lumi noted.

“That’s smart, Lumi,” Draco commended. “We could ask him or his boss, Celestia.”

“Will they allow us in the building?” Arka asked.

“Sure.” Draco pulled the note out and showed it to them. “I mean, he said I could visit him and maybe even do some jobs for them, so they must let us in. Right?”

“Well, we shouldn’t keep him waiting!” Lumi stuffed her sketchbook into her pink backpack and pulled out a bag of jumbo marshmallows. “I even brought snacks!”

“I must respectfully pass. I’m against processed sugar. As a concept,” Arka said.

Draco accepted a marshmallow and ate it as they began walking. After their run-in with the Guardian, Lumi regaled them with stories of the art she had created the night before.

“I felt so inspired after we learned to try new perspectives!” she exclaimed around a snootful of marshmallows. “I finished my painting and even started a whole new one!”

“I was able to add a new arm to my sculpture,” admitted Arka.

“My map design really started making more sense once I started looking at it differently,” Draco agreed with his friends. “Hey, Arka, this might be the summer you finally finish your sculpture.”

“Doubtful,” she sniffed. “It’s not perfect, but I know I can make it much better.”

As they approached the city, Draco noticed more dragons moving around them. He loved going into Downtown Everbright—a diverse array of dragons lived there, different from the ones in his neighborhood, and he loved to watch them as they walked by, living their own lives. Some of them had scale tattoos or many rings on their ears like Arka, or wore intricate pieces of shiny jewelry around their necks or wrists, signaling a sizable horde or a family of status.

“Are you ever gonna finish that thing?” Lumi asked Arka. “You’ve started it over completely, like, seven times. You could have made so many smaller sculptures by now.”

“Perhaps. Or perhaps it’ll never be done.” Arka tucked the tiny mechanism she’d been fiddling with into one of her many belt bags. “I’m completely alright with that. If it’ll never be perfect, then it shall never be finished.” Her mouth twisted, showing a flash of fang. Draco knew the idea of never finishing the sculpture bugged her, but Arka was too proud to admit that.

Draco had heard plenty about Arka’s perpetual sculpture over the years. She’d been working on it as long as they’d known each other, possibly longer. One day, when Arka was a little older, maybe she could put it down, or maybe one day she would deem it finished, and it would win a hundred awards. Either way, Draco had seen the sculpture many times and always really liked it, but it never looked like the same piece of art.

“We support you either way,” Draco told her.

“Thank you, Draco, I appreciate that,” Arka said, a soft smile playing on her lips as she acknowledged the support from her friend.

Just past the gates that led into Downtown, where the buildings started to get more crammed together, the Flametail Design office building loomed. It was a sleek, silver, boxy tower that seemed to scrape the sky, with many shining windows. The three dragonlets squeezed down an alley between two buildings as a shortcut, and then the building was right in front of them. As they got closer, Draco could see that there were barely any plants or trees, and the ones that remained were hedges trimmed within an inch of their lives.

"Hello," one of the guards outside ventured as Draco and his friends approached. He and his coworker on the other side of the door wore badges that marked them as security guards. "What is your business here?"

"I'm here to see my dad," Draco peeped, less sure that he would be let in now with these two burly, menacing guards towering over him. "His name is... *Ignisar.*"

"You don't sound sure of that," the other guard said, crossing her arms. Arka stood up straighter, crossing her arms as well and shooting the two guards her best-unimpressed look. She noted this but only smiled a bit, not threatened at all. "He doesn't seem sure. You sure that's his name?"

"Oh, he's sure," Lumi piped up, popping another marshmallow in her mouth. "You guys are just scary looking."

The two guards glanced at each other, and both let out loud, booming laughs. "We're just messing with you," the second guard said. "Check the list, Orion. He would have put them in for temporary entry passes."

Draco held his breath as the first guard, Orion, pulled a scroll out of his belt and scanned it. His dad was a bit forgetful. Hopefully, he remembered to put them on the list, or this adventure would be over quicker than he had thought.

"Names?" Orion asked them.

"We are Draco, Lumi, and Arka," Draco said.

He turned to the second guard. "Yep, they're on here."

The second guard leaned over and pushed the front door open. She said, "The elevator's out of order, so you'll have to take the stairs. Look for the metal door at the end of the hallway. I hope you're up for it—there are 15 flights. The floor below the penthouse is where you're headed. Do not go to the top floor."

"Why not?" Arka asked, dropping her defensive facade in pursuit of knowledge.

The guard raised her scaly brows, still amused. "Classified. Now hurry in before I change my mind."

"Oh, right," Draco said, nodding quickly as he motioned for his friends to follow. "Let's go, guys."

They were greeted by a rush of cool air as they entered the lobby. It was just as silvery and sleek as the outside, designed with lots of natural light from the picture windows. A few doors were lining the walls, and different designs and art pieces were hung above them. A spiral pattern was etched into the floor tiles that made Draco feel like he was being hypnotized.

"This artwork... it's creatively well done," Arka mused, glancing around at the walls. "It follows all the principles. The repetition of these shapes around the border, leading to the central figure, creates a great sense of unity. I love unity. You guys know my room is almost perfectly symmetrical. But there's no asymmetry to balance it, no mess. All of these pieces are like that. It all feels exactly the same."

"Like a robot did it," Lumi said. She offered the bag of marshmallows to Draco, and he shook his head, too nervous to eat.

Everything felt like it was closing in on him, like the cave walls, except everything was shiny, bright, and almost too perfect.

Draco remembered visiting his dad's office quite a few times when he was younger, always with his mom at his side. Back then, he was too young for school and far too young to be left alone. He was always with his mom as she went out on errands. He'd catch glimpses of the bustling lobby from the safety of his DragonWagon as they made their way to his dad's floor. The lobby didn't seem as polished or uniform as it did now, and the art on the walls used to be different, often featuring a great selection of works by various designers throughout the firm. Draco noticed that his dad's pieces were nowhere to be found.

"This place gives me the freaky deakies," Lumi said. Her voice echoed eerily in the pristine silence of the lobby.

"I agree," Arka said. "Where are all of the employees?" she asked.

As Draco, Lumi, and Arka walked through the halls of the enormous office, they noticed the eerie stillness around them. Desks that should have been cluttered with sketches and tools sat immaculately clean, and the usual hum of dragon's creatively working was replaced by an unsettling silence. It was as if the very life had been drained from the place.

Draco looked around nervously, trying to reconcile his memories of the vibrant, chaotic space with the sterile environment they now walked through. As they passed a partially open door, Draco expected to see designers hard at work, but instead, there was only a single dragon staring blankly at a canvas. In the same room, a small meeting was in progress, but instead of the usual lively back-and-forth, the voices were hushed and mechanical. "We need to maintain Flametail's classic appeal while introducing a fresh, modern edge," one dragon said, his tone lacking the passion that once defined these project discussions.

Arka nudged Draco, her eyes narrowing with uncertainty. "Something feels off," she whispered. "I'm not sure what, but it's like they're just... going through the motions."

Draco nodded, feeling a chill run down his spine. His father had always spoken of Flametail Design with such pride, but now, the halls felt eerily quiet, the energy that once filled the place now replaced by an unsettling stillness. As they neared the stairwell leading to his dad's office, an inexplicable sense of dread settled over Draco, making his scales prickle.

He glanced around again, and realized there were no other

dragons in sight. The small windows in the doors revealed nothing but dark, empty rooms, and the flickering lights above cast long shadows across the cold floor. Another chill ran down his spine.

What was really going on here at Flametail Design?

The three friends came to a stop in front of the metal door at the end of the hallway. Draco's claws hovering over the handle. Behind it lay answers... or more questions. He took a deep breath, reached for the handle and pushed the door open.

Chapter 7
Celestia

The dragonlets stepped into the stairwell, the door closing behind them with a heavy thud that echoed through the enclosed space. Without hesitation, they began climbing the steps that spiraled upward, the narrow stairwell winding endlessly above them. With each flight, the shadows on the walls seemed to grow longer, twisting and flickering in the dim light, adding to the sense of unease that clung to the air.

"I was hoping this place had fewer stairs than it looked from the outside," Arka muttered. "It doesn't."

As they climbed higher, the air grew noticeably cooler. Draco felt a strange energy humming through the walls, making his scales prickle.

He glanced around as he ascended the seemingly endless steps. At first, he thought his mind was playing tricks on him after staring at the stairs for so long. But then he blinked, focusing. Letters—bright and almost glowing—began to appear on the walls. These weren't just ordinary letters. Each one was intricately designed, as if every stroke and curve had been carefully crafted to be a work of art in its own right.

They almost seemed to glow and were in bright colors that contrasted nicely with the otherwise dull paint.

"Hey, do you guys see those letters on the walls?" Draco asked, his voice colored with excitement.

"Letters?" Lumi squinted at the walls, but her eyes didn't catch anything in particular. "I don't see any letters," she sighed, her voice tinged with frustration.

"Me neither. Are you certain you're not just tired?" Arka asked, ever the logical one.

"No, these are different. They're, they're magical," Draco insisted. He reached out to touch one, and as his claw made contact, the letter shimmered and transformed into a word: Kerning. His knapsack started to buzz and hum. "What the...?" He pulled the Codex of Design out. It vibrated slightly, as if resonating with the magical typography, then fell open in his paws to a page in the middle of the book. The word on the wall vanished as the book opened, the title appearing at the top of the page—*Kerning*. Draco tried his best to read while still walking up the stairs. Arka grabbed one of his horns and used it to guide him.

"Kerning is the process of spacing two letters at a time, making them either further apart or closer, so that they appear visually appealing amongst the entire word and sentence."

"Oh." Arka's brow furrowed. "So, when I'm making one of my maps, and I space the title out at the bottom, so it fits evenly in the available space, I'm kerning?"

The book vibrated, emitting a low, displeased hum. Another word glowed on the wall, just as captivating as the first: Tracking. With a swift motion, Draco tapped the word with his claw, almost too eagerly. The letters spaced out in response before disappearing, and the page turned over on its own accord.

"Another word?" Lumi asked eagerly.

"Tracking is the process of spacing letters in an entire word, sentence, or paragraph, either further apart or closer. Tracking affects from as few as two characters to an entire block of text."

"I see. So, spacing out the entire title would be Tracking, but Kerning is the spacing between two letters of the word?" Arka said, getting nearly as invested as Lumi.

A thumbs-up popped up in the margins of the magical book.

There was another word in the book too—*Leading*.

"Leading, pronounced 'ledding,' is the spacing of lines of text, vertically, from baseline to baseline," Draco read aloud. "This term comes from the early days of printing with movable type, like with the Gutenberg press. Printers used thin strips of lead between lines of type to create spacing, hence the name. It's also called Line Spacing."

"Whoa, this is like interactive learning!" Lumi exclaimed. Though she couldn't see the letters the book referenced, she seemed excited nonetheless.

"It's more than that," Draco said thoughtfully. "I think these magical letters are guiding us. Kerning, Tracking, and Leading are all about creating harmony through the right spacing. And we're on a mission to bring harmony back to the design world. Maybe this is a clue to what we need to do next?"

"What do you mean by that?" Lumi asked.

"I dunno," Draco admitted with a shrug, his gaze dropping to the steps below. "But I'm sure we'll know when we get there."

"Speaking of getting there..." Arka glanced around the landing they found themselves on. They hadn't noticed when they passed the 14th floor, too focused on the seemingly never-ending stairs. Now, instead of another flight, the floor ended abruptly in a bare white wall with a single white door in the middle. A sign above the door read "Executive Suite."

To the side, under the dim light of the landing, rested a sizable desk. Though not particularly striking at first glance, the scattered papers and curious objects hinted at a figure of importance—someone who managed their affairs with both care and confidentiality.

Draco's eyes briefly took it in before focusing back on the door. "Looks like we went up a little too high," he said, realizing they had overshot his dad's floor. He turned to Lumi, who was staring wide-eyed at the mysterious door before them, practically gleaming with curiosity.

"Lumi, don't even think about it," Draco said, his tone firm yet laced with a hint of amusement."Ugh. No fun. Why not?" Lumi whined. "Just a peek won't hurt!" she insisted, her curiosity gnawing at her resolve.

"Maybe because the guards downstairs told us to our face that we were not, under any circumstances, supposed to go to the top floor?" Arka reminded her, disapproval written all over her scaly face.

“Well, I don’t think they said all that,” Lumi said.

“It was implied,” Arka insisted.

“We wanted to talk to Ms. Celestia, right?” Lumi turned to Arka, then Draco. “This is probably where she works, don’t ‘cha think?”

“Well, yeah, but can’t we just ask my dad to take us to her?” Draco asked. “We’re here to see him, not to snoop,” he added.

“What if he says no? And then he’s watching us like a hunter all day, and we won’t ever have the chance to talk to her,” Lumi said. She leaned forward slowly. “Just one little peek—” She put her paw against the door.

“Lumi!” Arka snapped, and Lumi stumbled in shock, pushing the door open all the way by accident. She windmilled her arms to stay upright. Arka reached out, trying to stop her as she fell, but missed grabbing her by barely a claw’s length.

Lumi seemed to fall in slow motion, and Draco was frozen, only able to watch it happen until what felt like several minutes later, Lumi fell flat on her snout inside the top floor that they were told very specifically not to go into.

“Well, there was no going back now,” Lumi said, taking a deep breath.

“Rats,” Draco whispered.

Arka tried to pull Lumi up hurriedly, Lumi’s claws skittering on the marble. “Perhaps no one saw us. Perhaps it’s just a hallway or—”

“I don’t think that’s the case,” Lumi squeaked. She finally stood up fully and gestured into the open doorway.

The three friends cautiously peeked their heads into a luxurious penthouse office. An elegant yet clearly confused silver dragon was seated at an imposing desk in the center.

“Oh,” Arka said, her voice trailing off in contemplation, “Or perhaps not.”

The silver dragon—presumably Celestia, although Draco had never actually met her before—stood, twinkling smoke spilling from her nostrils. “What is your business here?” she asked, tipping her round spectacles down on her snout so she could look over them at Draco and his friends. She didn't sound pleased to be asking that question.

"Um," Lumi said, her voice trailing off as she hesitated, her brows furrowed in uncertainty. "We're—" She struggled to find the right words.

"Interns!" Draco yelped. "Yes, we're... we're traveling interns. We're very young interns. Here to apply for an internship at your studio."

"I don't believe that is how interns work," Arka mumbled under her breath.

"Go with it," Draco hissed back.

Lumi bowed deeply. "Yeah, I mean, yes!"

"Why is your first instinct always to bow?" Arka asked in hushed tones. "She's not a queen."

Celestia moved closer. She was tall, towering above them, and wore an impressive amount of jewelry, all sleek and polished like the rest of the building. Draco imagined her hoard was ginormous, what with the amount of projects Flametail Design took on all over Draconia. She might as well have been a queen. There was a strange vibe from her that Draco didn't like.

"Interns?" Celestia mused. "We haven't put out a call for interns recently."

"We'll be out of your scales, then, ma'am," Arka said, turning to leave the office, but Celestia held up one paw, thoughtful. Several rings glittered on her claws. All three dragons froze in place, frightened.

"Yet... I sense potential. A drive," Celestia mused. She stepped closer to them, clasping her claws behind her back, jewelry jingling. "Ordinarily, this would be an unwelcome intrusion. I don't usually allow uninvited guests into my workspace," Celestia said, her voice cool but measured. "However, it must not have been easy to make it this far. Did you encounter any resistance along the way?"

"I wouldn't say that," Lumi said. Arka elbowed her. "Oof!"

Celestia shook her head. "Good security guards are hard to come by."

"It wasn't their fault. See... we're not actually interns. My dad works here," Draco blurted out. "...on the floor right below. He said you guys might need help around the firm. Help with designing things. And, well, it seems like such a cool place to work! So, we decided to try our paw and apply it here. And then we came to the wrong floor..." he trailed off.

Celestia peered at Draco and pushed her spectacles back up again. Something about her gaze... her eyes were dark, nearly pitch-black. They were piercing and cold. It felt like she was studying him, paging through his brain like Draco paged through the design book. A chill went down Draco's spine. "Ignisar?" she asked finally. "Is he your father?"

Draco nodded, blinking rapidly. "Yes."

"Ma'am," Lumi added helpfully.

"I see the resemblance... Yes, I've heard many things about you. Hopefully, his work ethic is hereditary. It'll be useful if I choose to hire you," said Celestia.

"Really?" Lumi exclaimed.

"I'll need resumés from each of you, of course," Celestia said. "And the interview process is... well, let's simply say it's gotten a bit more difficult recently."

"After the past few days we've had, it can't be that difficult," Arka murmured.

"We'll get to work on those right away, ma'am," Draco said.

"Wonderful. We could certainly use some young, fresh perspectives around here." Celestia looked up from her papers. "Well, I'm a busy dragon. Come back with resumés, and we'll set you up for interviews. How does that sound? I'll make sure the security guards do a better job of guiding you all next time. Speak to my assistant Grocklepot and he will help you with some forms."

"That sounds great," Arka said, shooting silencing glances at Draco and Lumi. "Thank you, Ms. Celestia."

"Now, I'm sure your dad would love to see you." Celestia went back to her work. It was a clear dismissal. Draco ushered his friends out, and they closed the door carefully behind them.

Lumi let out a giant breath. "Gosh! Well, I think that could have gone a lot worse. Don't you, Arka?"

"Hmph," Arka grumped. "You are fortunate you didn't get removed from the building. We all are."

"Where is this Grocklepot?" Draco asked, peering around them.

"Ahem," a voice said behind them.

The dragonlets turned around to see a small dragon seated at the large cluttered desk. The desk's size dwarfed him, emphasizing his small stature even more.

"Ms. Celestia asked us to speak with you about forms to fill in for an internship?" Arka said.

Grocklepot grunted and turned around to grab forms from a filing cabinet.

"Fill these in somewhere else. Be away with you! Ms. Celestia is very busy with the four relics... I mean... oh dear," Grocklepot's eyes went wide, realizing his slip. He immediately began to stammer, "Uh, I mean... floor tiles! Yes, we're very busy with some, uh, floor tile renovations!"

"Four relics?!" Draco's eyes narrowed, locking onto Grocklepot.

"Did I say relics? Silly me, I meant floor tiles! So many tiles to count, measure, and... arrange!" Grocklepot's voice cracked as he frantically tried to cover his mistake. He started waving his claws, shooing them away. "Now, off you go! Important tile business, very secretive, very boring!"

Draco exchanged a quick knowing glance with Lumi and Arka. Without another word, the three dragonlets turned on their heels and headed straight for the stairs. Whatever Grocklepot was hiding, they had to find out—immediately.

Chapter 8
Ignisar

"Come on, let's go talk to my dad," Draco said as they hurried down to the 14th floor, Grocklepot's panicked words still echoing in his mind.

Their claws clicked against the steps as they descended, and Draco couldn't shake the feeling that every step was leading them deeper into a mystery they weren't prepared for.

"Draco, do you see any more words?" Lumi asked, her voice hushed.

Draco looked; unfortunately, the glowing words had all vanished without a trace. New ones didn't seem to appear as they walked; not like they had popped into existence on the way up.

"Maybe they were leading upwards?" Draco offered, reaching for the floor handle right below the executive suite.

"If the book seems to know all, in a magical sense, why would it be leading us towards a place we aren't meant to go?" reasoned Arka. They followed Draco into the maze of office cubicles that made up his dad's floor.

Based on what they saw on the floors below, Draco was shocked to find designers working at desks and communal tables, chatting in low voices.

"Who says the office wasn't where we were meant to go?" Lumi said a little louder than she intended. Draco and Arka both quickly shushed her, but not in time to avoid dirty looks from other dragons at work.

"The security guards?" Arka shot back.

"Well, yeah, okay," Lumi huffed, quieter this time.

"I think I understand what you mean, Lumi," Draco said, dodging a few bespectacled dragons, some carrying stacks of papers and boxes of art supplies. "I don't think it was leading us to Celestia or her office, but maybe it was leading us to... I don't know... a way to hone our skills? And that's what this internship could be."

"I suppose," Arka relented.

Draco suddenly spotted a familiar pair of curling yellow horns, which were poking above a cubicle in the far-right corner. "Dad!" he hissed urgently in a whisper.

Ignisar's head popped up, looking around for the source of the voice. "Draco?" he called back quietly. Draco bounded over and hugged his dad, almost excitedly knocking the '#1 Dad' mug off his desk. "Careful, kiddo!" He laughed. "I'm not as young as I used to be," said his dad.

"Hello, Mr. Ignisar," Arka said.

"How's your day?" Lumi waved to him cheerfully.

"Well, hi, Arka, hi, Lumi. I'm good; I've just been busy today. And, well, every other day this week. Heh." And indeed, Draco's dad looked more rumpled than usual, his colorful tie coming loose and his giant, round spectacles going askew on his snout.

"We can come back later if you're in the middle of something," Draco offered, feeling suddenly guilty for cutting into his dad's work hours.

"Actually, you caught me at a good time. I'm in between projects as we speak," his dad said. "What can I help you with?"

"We saw Ms. Celestia!" Lumi exclaimed.

"What? Where and how did you bump into Celestia?" asked Ignasar, his curiosity piqued as he leaned forward, hoping for an explanation.

"It's kind of a long story," Draco started, but Arka interrupted him.

"We followed some glowing letters that only Draco could see, which led us to the top floor where Celestia works," she explained. "The story is actually quite short," Arka said.

"Well, I guess, but that's not what I meant," sighed Draco.

He hadn't wanted to explain all this to his dad. Prophecy stuff and magic stuff would only make him worry.

Ignisar's eyebrow ridges leaped up on his head in shock. "Draco, is that true?" he asked.

"Yeah?" Draco squeaked.

His dad's face betrayed no emotion for a few seconds. Draco felt a little nervous that his dad would be upset with him for breaking the company rules. Then he stood up, smiled, and clapped his son on the shoulder, and Draco relaxed. "Well, this whole time, I assumed you didn't have any magic—in my defense, you didn't show any signs of it—but this is great! Congratulations, Little Flame! We'll have to get you into some classes, of course, and tell your teachers so they can accommodate—"

"Dad," Draco interrupted. "That all sounds awesome, but I think the letters I was seeing are because of this." He pulled the book out of his bag and showed it to Ignisar.

"The Codex of Design," he read. "Interesting. Why do you think this lets you see those magic letters?" He opened it and paged through.

"I mean, just look at it," Draco said, gesturing at the book. "Some pages are blank, but some aren't, and they've been filling themselves in as we go."

"You kids and your imaginations," chuckled Ignisar, shaking his head. "Where did you get an empty book like this? Was it from that back-to-school sale they were having at Enchanted Embers Scrolls n' Quills? I said I'd leave you some money if you wanted to pick up supplies for..."

"What?" Draco snatched the book back from his dad and flipped through it. To his utter shock and chagrin, all of the pages were blank again. "No! There were things there, I promise!"

Arka took the book from Draco. "Fascinating!" She turned it upside down. "It seems everything we could see in here before has simply disappeared."

"Tell him, Arka! There were things in there," Draco pleaded. "A bunch of important things the Guardian probably wouldn't want us to lose..."

Arka peeked over the top of the book and nodded, confirming.

"Yup," Lumi chimed in. "You should have seen the map that was in there. Hoo, boy, it was something. I loved it, personally..."

Ignisar's brow furrowed as Lumi went on chattering. "I believe you, son," he interrupted, clearly playing along with the game and not actually believing what the dragonlets were saying. "I'm glad you three are having fun. It's a neat notebook. I'm sure you'll fill it up with some really detailed notes for your new magic classes."

"Perhaps he can't see it because he doesn't have magical abilities and is just an ordinary dragon," Arka offered.

"Hey now," Ignisar said mildly.

"Apologies."

"Well, I guess you can't help us with that." Draco tucked the book away with a sigh. He would be distraught with the magical item if it decided to show its contents later. "But we do have something you can help us with."

Ignisar turned around and sat back down in his creaky office chair. His desk was messy as usual, cluttered with different half-finished designs, measuring tools, paints, and calligraphy supplies. Framed photos of Draco hung on the felt walls, and a smiling cartoon dragon screensaver bounced across his clunky, old computer. Ignisar picked up his '#1 Dad' mug and sipped his coffee. "Of course, son"

"You know how you said the firm might have some extra work for us? Celestia wants to interview us and told us that she wants us to fill in these forms and some resumés." Draco gestured to his friends. "Well, none of us know how to do that."

"I have never had a job before," Arka admitted.

"Me either," Lumi said. "But gosh, it sounds like a lot of fun. Would we get a uniform? Or our own office for the job?"

"Maybe we should focus on getting hired first," Draco told her.

Ignisar perked up at the idea of being able to help them out with something. "I can definitely help you kids with that," he said.

Just then Grocklepot, Ms. Celestia's assistant sort of slithered silently next to them. "You are needed by Ms. Celestia immediately." He said to Ignisar and walked away.

Ignisar looked worried, "Stay here guys, I shall be back soon."

He walked away from the desks and disappeared after Grocklepot.

"What was that about?" Arka asked.

Draco shrugged. He didn't like this Grocklepot or Celestia.

The Codex of Design buzzed as if to agree and he took it out of his satchel.

Opening the pages, he saw a new note had been added which wasn't there before:

INVESTIGATE CELESTIA.

Chapter 9
Resumé Magic

Draco showed the note to Lumi and Arka.

"Investigate her? But how?" Lumi said.

"How is the Codex of Design writing these messages to us? Do you think it has anything to do with what the Guardian was telling us?" said Arka.

"I think it does. She said the book would be our guide, and you heard Grocklepot mention the four relics. Maybe they're here! What do you think?"

Before the friends could answer, Ignisar returned from his meeting with Celestia, his expression calm yet focused. "All okay," he reassured them as he walked across the office with a confident nod. "Let's get to work, shall we?" Ignisar's presence exuded a sense of authority and experience that immediately put the dragonlets at ease.

Although Draco and his friends had little work experience, Ignisar emphasized the importance of building strong portfolios. "In the world of graphic design, your portfolio is your most valuable asset," he explained, guiding them through the process with patience and expertise. "In the absence of real work, you can use personal projects, sometimes called 'passion projects,' to demonstrate your skills and knowledge."

Ignisar showed them how to compile their best work, arrange it effectively, and present it with confidence. His detailed instructions and encouragement helped the dragonlets understand the real-world applications of their skills and the significance of showcasing their creativity.

For Lumi's portfolio, she picked some of her favorite drawings and paintings out of her sketchbook. This was the first time Draco could really look at a collection of her work all in the same place. She drew everything: Draco recognized sketches of the Big Tree outside of their school, the front of Lumi's family home, pictures of her many siblings, and even paintings of Draco and Arka themselves. Draco was stunned by her knack for blending, shading, and especially color palettes, which looked beautiful and complemented each other in ways that made the works stand out.

"How do you know which colors to use?" Draco asked her, curious. He always agonized over what combinations of colors to design his pieces with, but Lumi never seemed to plan her colors—she just jumped in and used what felt right.

"Color theory, silly!" Lumi flipped to the end of her sketchbook and sat it on the desk. Painted on the cardboard of the back cover was a color wheel, showing off all of the colors of the rainbow in a neat circle, surrounded by doodles and smiley faces. "This triangle of colors here..." Lumi pointed to the wheel's red, blue, and yellow spots. "They're called primary colors, meaning you can make any color you want if you have all three of those paint colors. Oh, and white and black, of course. And every primary color has an opposite. Yellow has purple, red has green, and blue has orange. In designs, those colors look great together because they are complementary. They're total opposites, which is why it works! Isn't that cool?"

"I'm just astounded that your circle is so neat," Arka said. Her portfolio was sure to be full of small, perfectly symmetrical gadgets, geometrically pleasing designs, and photos of the different stages of her sculpture.

"I used a compass," Lumi admitted. "It's the thing that spins a pencil in a circle, not the thing that tells what direction you're going. But the color mixing was all me."

Arka turned to Draco. "What is your portfolio going to be like? Is there anything you want to focus on?"

Draco took out his notebook and sketchbook, including the map he had drawn the day before, along with a few other sketches. Those designs from school, like the sign he'd made advertising the Design Club bake sale or the flowchart for his History class. Or personal designs, like doodle pages of his friends playing games or the t-shirts and posters he made for the wall of his favorite rock band, Emberquake. He was proud of his work and even considered a lot of it to be perfect designs, but unlike Arka and Lumi, none of it really had anything to connect it all together. There was no specific type of design he did, and none of the elements really jumped out to him as unifying all the pieces together. Draco suddenly felt a little lost. His friends' portfolios were all so coherent, showing off specific aspects of each of their talents. His portfolio was just a bunch of random stuff. Excellent random stuff, but random nonetheless.

"Draco?" Lumi prompted.

He opened his mouth to answer, looking down at his work. "Dad," he said instead of answering the question. "Do you know where I could get a snack?"

Lumi, with a mischievous glint in her eye, slowly held a small crumbly treat in front of Draco's nose and whispered, "Pocket cookie," then giggled, clearly amused by her own humor. Draco waved it off with a half-smile.

"Sure, let's go to the staff room. They'll have something good." Ignisar rose from his chair and guided Draco towards the door on the other side of the room, past other dragons working in their own cubicles and dragons discussing design projects at small community tables, steaming coffees next to them as they drew and spoke.

"What did you want to eat?" Ignisar asked cheerfully. "I saw some cheese curls in there earlier. I know how you love your cheese curls."

"I didn't actually want anything to eat," Draco admitted. "I just needed to get away for a second," he murmured.

Ignisar nodded, his expression thoughtful and understanding, but remained silent as they continued walking. The corridor between the different work rooms was long and just as bland as the rest of the office. Draco felt increasingly uneasy with each step.

"Your friends are really talented," Draco's dad said finally.

"They are," Draco said. "I love them both, I really do, and I love seeing their art. But I'm a little jealous." He stopped in the middle of the hallway and put his head in his paws, sad smoke billowing out between his claws. "I feel like such a bad friend for saying that."

"Aw, no, son." Ignisar immediately pulled him into a hug. "You're not a bad friend," he assured him. "Everyone feels jealous of others sometimes. It's not something you can control. As long as you're not mean to them because of it, and you're happy for them, and you don't let it turn into resentment, there's nothing wrong with feeling something that every dragon sometimes feels."

"I dunno, Dad," Draco said, a bit depressed. "Lumi is so good with colors, and Arka is such a master of shapes, but I feel like I do a bit of everything."

"Well, a good graphic designer should have a handle on a wide range of disciplines," Ignisar said. "It's not bad to feel like your skills are spread out evenly. In fact, it's exactly what will make you a truly versatile designer."

"I understand that, but I just feel like I should have one thing I focus on, like Lumi and Arka do."

Ignisar thought for a second. "What are you most excited to incorporate into your designs?"

Draco sighed. An annoyed puff of smoke came out of his nostrils. "I really like it all. That's the problem!"

Draco's dad put a paw on his shoulder. "You're a very young designer, Draco. You shouldn't be expected to have a distinct style right away. Not while you're still learning all the different ways to be a designer. You just have to keep doing what makes you happy, son. And, of course, you have to learn the rules to break them accordingly."

Draco nodded, accepting this—accepting the fact that he was going to have to learn. "Okay."

"I think you're just as good as your friends are... if not better." Ignisar winked.

"Daaa-aaad." Draco nudged his dad gently in the ribs. "You're biased."

"Maybe just a bit," he said. "But I'm also correct. Now, about those cheese curls..."

Ignisar and Draco picked out some snacks and rejoined Lumi and Arka in the office block. Draco's friends had moved to an empty collaborative worktable and were now organizing their pieces into different piles, ready to assemble their portfolios.

Lumi looked up and grinned at the two of them as they approached. "Draco! I just saw your sketch of the playground at school, and I'm fully obsessed." She held it up and waved it around. Arka grabbed her wrist and made her slowly lower the piece to the table.

"Thanks, Lu." Draco pulled the drawing under his claw towards him, adding it to his portfolio stack.

Draco and his friends spent a couple more hours reviewing their art and sorting their best and not-as-good pieces for their portfolios. Once that was done, they moved on to making resumés. Halfway through, Ignisar excused himself to go to a meeting, fixing his glasses and letting them know he would put in a good word with Celestia as he ran off.

Draco had almost finished his resumé when Lumi released a low growl of frustration. "What's wrong?" Arka asked from across the table.

"Look at my resumé!" Lumi said, spinning it around towards Arka. Even upside down, Draco could see "RESLUMI!" in bright purple lettering at the top, covered in stickers.

"It's very... you," Arka said, tail flicking.

"I know, but look at Draco's!" she exclaimed, pointing at Draco's paper, where he was meticulously spacing letters to ensure they all fit evenly and look nice.

Before Draco could respond, the Codex of Design on the table flipped open as if caught by a magical breeze. The pages turned to a section about spacing, with the definitions of Kerning and Tracking lighting up excitedly.

"This must be why I saw the letters on the walls," Draco said, realization dawning on him. "The book is guiding us."

As he said this, the letters on Lumi's "RESLUMI" began to glow the same mystical blue. Draco reached out a claw to touch it, and just as he did, the letters lifted off the page and moved, jumbling into a pile in the corner before rearranging into proper spacing. The letters bounced like animated balloons, each one finding its perfect position with a little blue spark, as if to declare it's spot.

They all went quiet for a moment as the letters wobbled around. The aftershocks of Draco's claw had them moving slightly in their new places.

The three dragonlets stared in awe. "Did you just...?" Arka began.

"Push written letters on the paper?" Draco finished. "Yeah, I think I did. Do you see the sparks?"

"Yeah... do it again!" Lumi urged.

Draco repeated the process, spacing out the letters with his claw. This time, he focused on kerning three characters at a time, adjusting the spaces until the entire word looked balanced. Magical sparks flew from his claw, and as the letters settled into perfect harmony, each gave a declarative tiny explosion of blue sparks.

Draco started by looking at the first three letters of "**RESLUMI**", "**RES**," making sure the spaces between "**R**," "**E**," and "**S**" were equal. Then, he moved to the next set of three, "**ESL**," which included the last two letters from the previous step, and adjusted the spacing again. He continued this method, checking "**SLU**," "**LUM**," and finally "**UMI**," each time making sure the spaces were balanced. By the end, the entire word "**RESLUMI**" was evenly spaced and looked just right.

"Wow, Draco!" Lumi clapped. "It looks amazing now!"

Arka's eyes widened. "You have a gift, Draco. This is incredible!"

Draco smiled, still in awe of his newfound ability. "I guess I do. Thanks, Codex!"

The Codex of Design seemed to glow a bit brighter, as if acknowledging Draco's gratitude. The three friends shared a look of excitement and wonder, ready to see what other magical skills they could unlock.

Following along with the Codex of Design, Draco was sure the kerning on his friends' resumés was picture-perfect. He used his claw to push the letters around, adjusting them just as he had learned. Lumi still retained her bright colors and artful sticker placement, but the letters were now nicely spaced and much easier to read. Arka's resumé was elegant, but the spaces between her letters were much too wide, making it just as hard to read as Lumi's. Draco squeezed them together for her, creating a balanced and polished look.

Just as he was finishing up fixing Arka's resumé, the text in the Codex of Design began to blur and disappear, as if it were wet ink hit with a cup of water. Draco looked up in utter shock, only to realize his dad was coming back.

So, he wasn't crazy—the book didn't want his dad seeing what it said. Draco wondered if it was his dad in particular or maybe all adults.

Despite the initial shock, Draco felt a sense of relief. He wasn't as upset with the book as he thought he would be. Instead, he was grateful that the clues and teachings the Guardian was leaving for them were not lost forever, easing the fear he had felt earlier.

"Are you kids about ready to go home?" Ignisar called out.

Draco looked around and saw that, while he and his friends had been so absorbed in making their resumés and portfolios, the office block had been cleared out, except for a few dragons packing up their bags and briefcases, heading back to their houses for a long night's rest before coming back the next day to do it all over again.

Arka and Lumi took their portfolios and resumés, and the three dragonlets shared an apprehensive look. "Yeah, Dad," Draco said. "Let's go home," he added with a hint of reluctance in his voice.

Ignisar led them out towards the lobby, and the best friends went their own separate ways home, pensive, excited, and scared about what would become of them the next day.

Chapter 10
The Golden Ratio

"I've never heard of anyone dying during a job interview," Arka said. "However, that doesn't mean it's entirely impossible."

"You're such a worrywart," Lumi chided.

Draco and his best friends had met each other at the Big Tree once again and were walking towards Flametail Design for their interviews, which were to take place in about an hour. Lumi had slipped her portfolio into her sparkly pink backpack, Arka had hers under her arm, and Draco could feel the weight of his portfolio in his trusty knapsack.

"After this, what do you think the book will want us to do?" Lumi asked Draco.

"I'm assuming we'll do our jobs and investigate Celestia somehow," Draco said.

"We still haven't figured out what the map and the word SCHER really mean," Arka said, her gaze focused on the book. "It seems like the book is trying to lead us somewhere. And there's also that contest coming up."

Lumi looked puzzled. "What contest?"

Arka paused, then clarified, "The design contest hosted by the Everbright Design Council. Mentor Blaze kept reminding us about it last week."

Lumi's eyes widened with realization, her excitement clear. "Oh, that contest! It's such a big deal in the design world. How could I forget?"

Draco nodded, adding, "It feels like the book and the contest might be connected somehow. We could be onto something big."

"Oh!" Lumi exclaimed, scrunching up her snout. "I almost forgot about that!"

"We did find the book when we were looking for instructions on how to make a map," Draco realized. "Maybe that's its end goal? Do we need to make a map?" The book buzzed in his bag. It sounded angry, if a vibrating magical book could sound like anything. "Well, I guess that's a no."

"Is it going to tell us what it wants, or will it simply keep telling us we are wrong?" Arka directed this at the bag. The book said nothing.

The three dragonlets turned down the alley, the shortcut to get to Flametail Design Studios. It seemed even darker than it had the day before and almost too quiet. Draco thought he saw figures lurking at every turn but convinced himself it was all his imagination. That is, until one of them stared right back at him.

"Hey, guys..." Draco started nervously, backing into Lumi. He watched as a shadow began to move towards him, claws outstretched. It was a dragon dressed in all black, a mask pulled low over their snout like a burglar in a cartoon movie.

More shadows began to stir, revealing dragons emerging from the dark corners of the alley, all dressed in identical cloaks. Draco's heart pounded furiously as fear gripped him. They were surrounded, and in danger.

"Hey, guys, what's going on?" Lumi asked cheerfully, seemingly oblivious to the threat looming around them.

Arka, however, was already on alert. Her gaze fixed on the shadowy figures as she rummaged in her belt bag, searching for something—maybe a weapon. But Draco knew it wouldn't matter; there were too many of them. Three dragons were circling them now, their silent approach tightening the noose around the trio.

Draco swallowed hard, his mind racing. They had to find a way out, but the alley felt like it was closing in on them.

The lead dragon opened their mouth, eyes glinting as if about to speak or cast a spell. But Draco wasn't willing to give them a chance.

"Run!" howled Draco, sprinting towards the alley's exit. His wings unfurled with a powerful snap, catching the air and lifting him partially off the ground with every stride. Each flap sent gusts of wind swirling around him, propelling him forward with bursts of speed as his paws pounded the cobblestone street.

He could hear Arka's heavy footfalls close behind and Lumi's breathless questions echoing in the narrow alleyway, her voice rising in panic with every step. "What if they want the book? Or worse, what if they're just really bad at making friends?"

The three friends sprinted towards the entrance of the Flametail Design building. The dark dragons followed their forms, weaving through the air like shadows pursuing the light. The guards saw them coming and opened the doors for them, pulling out their batons to fend off the dragons chasing them. As the young dragons reached the entrance, they scrambled inside, their hearts beating wildly.

After they finally reached safety, Lumi collapsed onto the cool tiles of the floor, rolling onto her side and resting her head against the ground. "That was terrifying!" she wheezed, her wings trembling slightly as they settled back against her body.

Draco, Lumi, and Arka all turned their heads in unison towards the picture windows, watching the dragons swoop at the building like dark birds diving for prey. They pulled up and zoomed off at the last second, leaving the door guards shaking their batons skyward at nothing.

"They're running," Arka noted. She seemed completely unruffled despite sprinting several hundred feet at top speed while Draco and Lumi sat on the ground in the lobby and tried to catch their breath.

"That was worrying," Draco said.

"What's worrying?" A familiar voice spoke behind them. Draco, his friends all whirled towards it in unison. Ms. Celestia had appeared in her lobby, seemingly out of nowhere, Draco's dad trailing behind her.

"We were attacked!" Lumi blurted it out.

Draco and Arka hissed at her.

Celestia raised her eyebrows, tipping her glasses down on her snout. "Attacked? Is this true?" Celestia asked.

"Yes, we were on our way over and someone came out of the shadows at us!" Draco admitted.

"They've gotten so much bolder," Ignisar murmured to himself. Celestia shot him a look, and he went quiet immediately.

Draco felt Arka shift next to him, making a small noise of curiosity, and Draco knew it wasn't just him who had caught the interaction. "What, Dad?" ventured Draco.

Ignisar shook his head, staying silent.

"Never you mind," Celestia said with a reassuring smile. "It's time for your interview. That is if you feel you're ready and aren't too shaken up by today's events." Her gaze softened, conveying encouragement.

"We are ready," Arka said, confident as always, though a flicker of doubt crept into her voice.

Celestia turned to the security guards. "Make sure those dragons don't get in here," she told them with a flick of her tail. "Tell the other guards to end their break early. Use any force necessary." She headed back towards the stairs without another word.

Ignisar gestured for the dragonlets to follow them. Arka and Draco picked Lumi up off the floor, and, with no small amount of groaning and grumbling, they followed.

"Are you ok, son? Are your friends all right?" Ignisar said as they walked.

"Dad, we are fine, but it was scary."

To their surprise, when they reached the stairwell, Celestia headed down the stairs instead of up. "Your first challenge is located in the basement," she called over her shoulder. "I'm quite busy, so I will ask your father to explain it to you, and after you complete the challenge, you will meet me upstairs for the second part of your interview."

"What's happening?" Lumi murmured to Arka.

"What's the challenge?" Arka shrugged.

Draco and his friends met at the bottom of the stairs, standing on a cold concrete floor with a towering wall looming in front of them, made of the same material as a cubicle divider, but with a single narrow opening. The basement was dim, and the angular, modern steel sconces flickered with harsh white light that barely reached the room's far corners. Even when Draco craned his head, he couldn't see where the room ended.

"Well," Celestia said brightly. "I must be off." In a flash of white light, she vanished quicker than her shadow could follow.

"Interesting!" Arka ran to the spot where Celestia had vanished, peering at the unassuming concrete patch. "How did she do that? I must ask her later."

"If this interview doesn't kill us," Lumi roared, eyeing the canvas wall before them as if it held secrets more perilous than the questions awaiting them.

"Who's the worrywart now?" Arka shot back.

"I didn't know there would be a maze involved!" Lumi hissed.

"It's a maze?" Draco asked.

"Hmm." Arka paced back and forth in front of the entrance. Her wings flapped once, and with a mighty gust, she lifted off the ground far enough to see over the wall. This was when Draco realized the wall didn't reach all the way to the ceiling; a gentle press of one of his paws confirmed the wall was temporary and seemed to have been placed there specifically for this test.

He turned back to Ignisar. "Dad?" he ventured.

"Oh. Yes." Ignisar pulled a crumpled piece of parchment from the pocket of his suit and his reading glasses and cleared his throat, a bit of smoke puffing from his nostrils. "Today, you embark on a quest to test your wits and teamwork. Within the maze lies the Golden Ratio, a source of great power. It is your task to find it."

"The Golden Ratio?" murmured Arka. "That sounds familiar. I can't quite recall..."

Ignisar nodded. "The Golden Ratio, mmm. That's what it says on this instruction sheet." He kept reading. "'The Golden Ratio is a fundamental principle of balance and harmony. It is hidden within the maze to teach you the importance of equilibrium in your powers and decisions.'"

Lumi bounced on her talons, the eagerness in her eyes igniting like wildfire. "This sounds like fun! Let's find that Golden Ratio thingy!"

Draco nodded in agreement. "I'm ready. Let's prove to Celestia that we're up to the challenge."

"That's all I have to tell you, according to the page." Ignisar pointed to the entrance of the maze. Draco peered in. "You kids will do just fine. Arka, your intelligence will guide the way. Draco tells me you have a brain for proportions, and I'm sure you've completed hundreds of mazes. Lumi, your positivity will keep everyone's spirits high. A joke or compliment can sometimes light up even the darkest passage. Draco, your determination will lead the charge. I can tell I've seen you make decisions under duress, and your friends trust you. Together... you form a great team."

"Thanks, Dad." Draco wrapped his arms around him and hugged him. Ignisar patted him on the back and the three friends entered the maze.

The door closed behind, darkness swallowing them.

They were alone and didn't know what was ahead, only they couldn't turn back.

Chapter 11
Further into the Maze

As they stepped into the maze, the wide open space of the first room made them all stop in their tracks. The ceiling rose high above them, supported by grand pillars that disappeared into the shadows. The sheer size of the space made Draco feel small, like a speck in a giant's lair.

"Now, that's a big room," Lumi whispered, her voice bouncing off the walls and echoing through the room. "How are we supposed to find anything in here?"

Arka, always the thinker, squinted up at the towering pillars and intricate designs carved into the walls. "These carvings feel purposeful," she whispered to herself, "like they're hiding something." She muttered a little louder, "We just need to figure out what it is."

The three dragonlets ventured deeper into the first room, their footsteps soft on the smooth stone floor. The space felt endless, with shadows stretching far beyond what their eyes could see. Every so often, Draco would glance at the walls, trying to find some kind of clue, but everything looked the same.

After what felt like an eternity, they reached the other side of the room and found a doorway leading into another chamber. This one was still large, but not nearly as vast as the first.

"This one's smaller," Draco observed. "But not by much."

Arka nodded, her sharp eyes scanning the space. "It's smaller, but it's still part of the pattern. We need to keep exploring."

They continued onward, room after room, each one smaller than the last. The changes were subtle at first, but by the time they reached the fourth chamber, they could clearly tell that the space was shrinking around them. The ceilings were lower, the walls closer, and the once-grand pillars were now simple columns of stone.

"This is getting weird," Lumi said, her voice tinged with

nervousness. "Everything's getting tighter, but I still don't see anything that looks like the Golden Ratio."

Draco frowned, feeling the weight of the maze pressing in on them. "I don't get it. We've been wandering for ages, and we're not any closer to finding the Golden Ratio. What if we're missing something?"

The book in his knapsack buzzed again, more insistently this time. Draco sighed and pulled it out, flipping to the section that had filled in with magical text. His eyes skimmed the page, and he read aloud: "The Golden Ratio is a special number, about 1.618. It's used in design to create balance and beauty. You'll often find it in nature, in things like shells and flowers, where the spacing follows this perfect proportion."

Arka's eyes lit up. "That's it! The Golden Ratio is all about balance, right? So maybe the maze is following that same principle. The rooms are shrinking in proportion to each other."

"But how do we know for sure?" Lumi asked, looking around and realizing that the room they're in, has grown encreasingly more cramped.

Draco pondered for a moment. Then, a thought struck him. "Maybe we need to see it from a different perspective. If we're stuck down here, we might be missing the bigger picture."

Without waiting for a response, he spread his wings and took off, soaring upward toward the ceiling. Lumi and Arka followed him, their wings flapping as they hovered near the top of the chamber. From above, the maze looked completely different—what had seemed like random rooms now formed a distinct spiral pattern.

"It's like a shell!" Draco exclaimed, pointing down at the layout. "The rooms are arranged in a spiral, and each one is smaller than the last. That's the Golden Ratio!"

Lumi peered down at the maze, her eyes wide with realization. "You're right! We've been walking through it this whole time."

Arka nodded, her mind racing. "Each room appears to be 1.618 times smaller than the one before it. That's the key to the Golden

Ratio. We just needed a different perspective to see it."

They descended back to the ground, excited by this newfound knowledge. "So, what now?" Draco asked, looking around the chamber and eyeing the other door.

"We follow the pattern to the center," Arka replied, pointing across the room, her voice filled with confidence. "Now that we know the secret, we can navigate the rest of the maze."

But just as they were about to press forward, the air around them went still, then shimmered. The soft glow of the chamber seemed to brighten. Out of the glow, Celestia appeared before them, her movements smooth and graceful, as though she had simply materialized from the shadows. A small, approving smile played crookedly on her lips, though her eyes gleamed with something far more complex than simple praise.

"Well done, young ones," she said in a voice that dripped with pleasant surprise. "You've unraveled the secrets of my maze—something very few have been able to do. Truly impressive." She paused, letting the words hang in the air, her gaze lingering on each of them in turn.

Her smile widened, though it didn't quite reach her eyes. "But remember, this is just the beginning. There are far more intricate puzzles and challenges ahead. If you continue with this level of dedication, who knows what you might achieve?" Her tone was sweet, but there was an underlying sharpness, like the edge of a blade hidden beneath silk.

"You've proven yourselves... so far. Let's see how far you can truly go," she added, her words both a compliment and a warning.

Celestia's smile lingered for just a moment before her expression shifted, becoming more formal and measured. "Now, the time has come for the next test," she announced, her voice was now calm but firm. "I require you to present your portfolios."

Draco's heart skipped a beat. He hadn't expected the request to come so soon. Celestia's gaze sharpened, focusing intently on each of them in turn, and the air seemed to grow heavier with the weight of her expectations.

"Follow me," Celestia continued, gesturing with a slight tilt of her head. "We will continue this discussion in my office."

Without saying another word, she extended her wing in a graceful yet commanding motion. Draco instinctively reached for Arka's claw, who took Lumi's in turn. With a gentle but firm touch, Celestia placed a claw on Draco's shoulder.

In an instant, the maze vanished around them, replaced by the cool, imposing interior of Celestia's office. The transition was seamless, as if the entire maze had been nothing more than an illusion. The three dragonlets stood in silence, still holding claws, as they took in their new surroundings.

Celestia went to stand behind her desk. "You have all passed the physical challenge with flying colors. Not many dragons your age have a grasp of the Golden Ratio. Now, I'm eager to see what creativity you bring to the table in terms of your own designs."

The three friends looked at each other in apprehension, having a silent staring battle to see which would take the plunge. Draco didn't care when he went, honestly... he just didn't want to go first.

Arka sighed and stepped forward first, pushing her portfolio across the desk to Celestia. Draco knew her portfolio showcased intricate geometric designs, angular sculptures, and mesmerizing patterns that danced across the pages.

"Ms. Celestia, I'm passionate about the beauty of angles and symmetry and how math can work hand in hand with graphic design," Arka said. She was trying to contain her excitement but loved talking about her sculptures so much that she almost bounced from claw to claw, just like Lumi. "I believe geometric designs can evoke a sense of order and elegance, especially in three dimensions."

She offered Celestia a few of the things she'd been fiddling with across the desk. Draco could see now that they were miniature sculptures of different items: a bird made of twisted scrap plastic, a tiny typewriter composed of mostly machine parts, and a ridged cornucopia with mini sheet metal fruits.

Celestia examined Arka's work with an approving nod. "This is impressive, Arka. Your geometric prowess reflects a unique perspective. A rational, organized mind like yours can be one of a dragon's greatest strengths. And these sculptures... they're very, very creative. You have an eye for the little things and a heart for details."

Next up, Lumi offered her work. Her pink portfolio revealed a breathtaking collection of paintings, sketches, and doodles, each bursting with vibrant colors and emotion. Landscapes, dragons, creatures, realism and cartoons, and abstract art were only a few of the things she had to offer.

"I love the harmony of colors, Ms. Celestia," Lumi shared, her eyes shining. "I want every brushstroke to tell something different, like a story! I think a splash of color can breathe life into any design."

"Agreed!" Celestia admired Lumi's paintings. Draco hoped she recognized the talent that spilled across each canvas. "Your understanding of color is exceptional, Lumi. The palettes, the hues, the command of light, negative spaces, and the blending all add a new dimension to our design possibilities. Well done."

Last in line was Draco. Too late, he wondered if going last had been the best idea in the world. Now, he had to go after both of his extremely talented friends. He swallowed his insecurity and handed Celestia his portfolio. Celestia opened it and examined the things Draco had assembled: his posters, his maps, his samples and ideas for new fonts, and his own drawings and sketches.

"I haven't found my specialty in design like these two have yet," Draco admitted, his wings twitching nervously. "My style is all over the place sometimes. But I want to learn. I think every facet of graphic design is so cool... but I believe words can convey powerful messages when presented with the right style and phrased correctly."

Celestia examined Draco's samples. "I notice there are a lot of text designs here. Typography is a vital aspect of design, Draco. Your exploration shows promise. Keep honing your skills and you may find your words shaping the very future of this world." Her statement sent chills down Draco's scaly spine. "Where Lumi and Arka have impressive eyes for detail, I can definitely use a dragon who appreciates the bigger picture more than anything."

"Thank you, ma'am," Draco said, unsure if this was a compliment or not.

Celestia leaned back in her chair, a silvery smile gracing her majestic features. She interlocked her claws, forming a pointed arch. "You've each shown exceptional creativity and prowess for your young ages. Arka, Lumi, Draco—welcome to Flametail Design." The three friends glanced at each other in excitement and breathed tandem sighs of relief. They'd done it!

But for some reason, Draco sensed something dark in Celestia. Like she had meant for them to pass the first test on Golden Ratio and even give them a job to keep them quiet... Did she know they had the book?

Chapter 12
The Midnight Shadows

"I look forward to seeing your talents blossom within our team," Celestia continued. "You may report back here tomorrow, and we will set up a schedule for you three for the rest of the summer, at the very least." She nodded toward the door. "I'll send word to your father. Unfortunately, he has a lot of important work to do, so you won't be able to reach him today." She gave a wicked grin and dismissed the dragonlets with a flick of her silver claw.

Draco nodded, disappointed but understanding. His dad was a busy guy. He couldn't wait to talk about his interview with him, though, no matter how late he got home that night.

Outside, it was already getting dark. The interview had taken longer than the three dragonlets had expected. They made their way downstairs to the front doors and saw the sun dipped low in the sky, casting a warm orange glow over the sprawling landscape as Arka, Lumi, and Draco made their way home from Flametail Design. The trio realized slowly they had just aced their interview, and the three of them couldn't help but chatter excitedly to each other as they walked.

Draco led the way, thinking of how his home would soon be filled with warmth and laughter. They had a good couple of hours before Arka's grandmother and Lumi's parents would start looking for them, so Draco seized the opportunity to invite them over for dinner. He was determined to try cooking spaghetti, though he joked about the risk of a culinary catastrophe. But the real comfort was in knowing they would share laughs and good times, whether things turned out perfectly or not.

"Can you believe Ms. Celestia liked our portfolios?" Lumi bubbled with enthusiasm, her blue scales shimmering in the fading light. "I never thought our designs would be good enough for her! I mean, jeez, she's scary. I thought she might bite our heads off, but instead, she basically told us that we rocked. What an unbelievable triumph!"

Arka nodded in agreement thoughtfully. She was already working on a new mini sculpture, barely looking down as she fiddled. "This is, I think, a great opportunity for us. Our hard work paid off, but we mustn't let it get to our heads. There's still much to learn and improve upon."

Draco flashed a grin, proud of himself and his friends. "Yeah, but we make a pretty awesome team, don't we? We didn't find out who Scher is or about the four relics. But Grocklepot did say that Celestia was busy with them..."

The two others made noises of agreement.

As they rounded the corner, their conversation was cut short by the sudden appearance of a mysterious figure. They stopped in the street between two large, looming buildings. A dragon, cloaked and wearing a black mask, emerged from the shadows cast by the building on the right. The masked stranger had the same build as the dragon that had led the group earlier, and Draco froze in place. It had to be the same dragon—it was too much of a coincidence for it not to be.

"Why are you following us?" Draco shouted.

"Because, what the heck," the hooded figure said indignantly. Draco recoiled in surprise. He sounded a lot younger than Draco had originally expected. Older than him and his friends, but still pretty young. "Why did you guys avoid the alley?"

"Maybe because you tried to jump us last time we went through there?" Lumi shot back.

"What?" he cried. He somehow looked offended even though Draco could only see part of his face, his red-scaled mouth twisting downward. "That wasn't what that was at all." He glanced around and then lowered his voice. "I can't remove my mask here to prove it, though. You gotta come with us."

Arka scoffed, crossing her arms. "And why on Draconia would we do something so imbecilic?"

Then the masked figure uttered the last words Draco ever thought they would say.

"It's because we know about the book."

"What book?" Draco said slowly.

"Your book. Don't be stupid," the masked dragon responded. "The book you got from the Secret Section at the library. The Guardian? The four relics? Ringing any bells? We can help you with that whole mess."

"Little bro." Another voice boomed from the shadows, deeper and older. "You're simply scaring them." Two more hooded, masked dragons appeared, evening the odds. One of them, the one who seemed to have spoken, was red as well, but a darker ruby red, and was much bigger and more muscular. The other dragon was violet and of medium build, and she wore crooked, bottle-thick glasses over her mask. "Hey, there, young ones," the deep red stranger's voice rumbled with an edge of mystery. "Good to finally meet you."

The trio of dragonlets exchanged wary glances, their instincts on high alert.

"That was wicked cool," Lumi said, her eyes wide with fascination. She didn't seem all that concerned, just really impressed by how they had made their entrance.

Draco's grip tightened on the strap of his satchel over his shoulder, where the enchanted book nestled snugly against his side.

"How do you know about our book?" Arka asked, her voice tinged with suspicion.

The ruby red dragon chuckled roguishly. "Let's just say we move in circles where information flows freely."

"Pardon my interuption, but we should speak privately," the violet dragon announced, glancing around. "There are too many hidden vantage points out here in the city. There could be booby traps, spies in the shadows..." She trailed off, eyes darting from shadow to shadow.

"Like you guys?" Lumi said.

"Exactly," the larger red dragon said with a deep laugh.

Arka nodded appreciatively at the violet dragon's sentiments.

"You're absolutely right, but these two never take me seriously when discussing vantage points."

"Booby traps are a matter of life and death!" the violet dragon exclaimed. Draco could see Arka softening where she was wary before, intrigued by someone similar to her.

"We can move to a safer place," the smaller red dragon piped up. "There's a warehouse, not two streets over from here."

"...the old FlynnWare building?" the violet dragon said, tapping a claw against her chin. "Yes, there are not a lot of hidden crevices there... it was a manufacturing facility for high-end gaming consoles. It's perfectly safe for a gathering, by my calculations."

"Like... a haunted arcade?" Lumi peeped, half worried, half joking as usual.

"Hold on!" Draco cried. "Who said we were going with you?"

"I mean, don't you want to know what's up with your book? Don't you want to know more about the four relics?" the smaller red dragon shrugged.

"I guess so," Draco admitted.

"No obligation, honestly," they said. "If you don't like our sales pitch, we'll leave you alone. But it'll take a while before you figure out what's going down without our help."

Draco glanced at his friends. Arka was still studying the violet dragon, and she was studying Arka, too. They were kind of slowly circling each other. Lumi was trying her best to hide behind Arka without it seeming obvious. They looked back at Draco. Lumi nodded uncertainly, and Arka gave a small, reassuring smile.

Draco looked back at the three new dragons. "Okay," he said. His voice only shook a little. "We'll hear you out," he assured them.

"Blazin'," the smaller dragon said, and without further ado, swept their cloaks over their shoulders and headed off between the buildings. It was hard to follow them, what with the entire city being cast in shadow from the lack of sun and the dark clothes they were wearing, but the three cloaked dragons always made sure to turn back and check to see if Draco and his friends were following close.

About three blocks over in the industrial district stood an abandoned warehouse. Draco had walked by it a few times, taking the long road to his dad's work, but he always tried to avoid it since it seemed a bit creepy. The kids at school theorized it was haunted, and some of them even swore they heard voices from behind the boarded-up door. Now Draco realized, as the dark-clothed dragon trio stealthily flew up to one of the broken windows and began wriggling in, that maybe they had encountered the ghosts themselves.

"Let's follow," Draco decided, watching the three other dragons deftly avoid the shattered glass and wires poking out around the window. They should probably hurry, or else they'd have no clue how to enter the warehouse without stabbing themselves accidentally.

"Are we positive?" Arka said, eyeing the broken-down building looming darkly in front of them. "No crevasses for hidden spies also means no sort of backup for us."

"We should hear them out," Lumi offered. "What's the harm? If they don't have any new stuff to tell us, we can just fly off home and eat spaghetti. I like late-night spaghetti, and I like home. Problem totally solved."

"We've been flying blind up to this point." Draco pulled the book from his satchel and held it up before him. "Have any advice for us on this front?" The book stayed stubbornly mute.

"Maybe it only talks about things like color theory and not a masked crew of dragons who could equally help or hurt us," Arka said.

"We'll never know unless we try," Lumi said.

Draco sighed, knowing both of his best friends were right in their own way. "I'll lead."

He took a running start, and just before he reached the base of the building, he leaped and flapped his wings. He misjudged the distance a bit, and with a yelp, he scrabbled at the windowpane for purchase, almost impaling his claws on a spike of broken glass barely hanging onto the frame.

"Jeez," he murmured to himself. He poked it with his spiny tail, so it dislodged from the frame and fell onto the top of one of the concrete pillars. Shuffling around slowly in a circle, he looked back down at his friends and called, "Come on, guys!"

Arka looked up at the edge of the window apprehensively. Lumi gave a claws-up and sprinted right at the wall like Draco had. "Incoming!" she yelled, and with a flap of her wings, half-flew, half-barreled up the side of the wall like a pastel spider. She just barely made it to the windowpane, and Draco was able to grab her and pull her up. They wiggled through to the ledge right below it.

Lumi was so close to falling and she didn't even realize it!

Chapter 13
Paula Scher and the Secrets of the Codex

Lumi let out a loud, dramatic yell and made it progressively quieter. Then she made an explosion noise with her mouth as if she had fallen all the way to the floor.

"Not funny, Lumi," called Arka crossly. With a whoosh of air, she lifted off and perched neatly on the windowsill above them, the picture of balance despite being much longer than both Draco and Lumi.

"Yo!" The younger red dragon called from the floor. "What part of 'secret' and 'quiet' did you halfwits not understand?"

Draco and his friends flew down to meet them, gingerly avoiding any detritus on the floor. He looked around at the warehouse they had finally entered. Its once vibrant walls now bore the scars of neglect, decorated with graffiti tags that told tales of forgotten friendships and long nights. The floor was wide, echo-y, and empty, save for debris from broken windows, the crumbling second floor, and a makeshift table fashioned from an old door propped up on crates.

Inside, among the echoes of the past, gathered the six young dragons. Arka paced around the dusty floorboards, her scales shimmering in the faint light that filtered through shattered windows.

"So, who exactly are you guys?" Lumi asked, cocking her head to the side.

"My name is Raze." The larger red dragon stepped forward, nodding to the smaller red and violet dragon. "This is my baby brother, Roth, and our friend, Cipher. The three of us represent a group known as The Midnight Shadows."

Arka's brow furrowed with curiosity. "The Midnight Shadows?" Arka inquired.

"Sounds sketchy," Lumi commented.

"What do you want with us?" Arka asked.

Roth leaned in, his eyes gleaming with excitement. "We're a rebellion, a group of dragons who're challenging the status quo, pushing the boundaries of creativity."

"Something is happening to the Everbright Design Council," Raze said. "We think your new boss, Celestia, has something to do with it and the missing four Relics of Design. And we know that your book holds secrets that could change everything."

Draco's heart pounded with uncertainty as he processed all this information, torn between curiosity and caution. "What kind of secrets?"

Raze's grin widened. "It's the kind that could reshape the design world as we know it. Join The Midnight Shadows, and together, we'll unlock the true power of your magic book. Help us help you."

"I don't know about this," Arka said.

"SCHER," Cipher blurted out. Draco and his friends whipped their heads around to stare at her, and she seemed startled. "Sorry. Sorry. Ok, that was loud." She adjusted her glasses self-consciously.

"How do you know that word?" Arka asked her.

"Like I said," Raze cut in, "we have our sources. We still work closely with the Guardian, and we've been investigating some disturbing developments. We discovered information about an ancient ritual, and we know Celestia is involved somehow. We've been monitoring her movements for weeks but haven't been able to get near Flametail Design."

"One second." Draco pulled his friends aside and lowered his voice. "What do we think?"

"They know about SCHER," Lumi said. "They also know the Guardian, Celestia, and the four relics. How do they know about those things if they aren't being honest?"

"Or this entire book situation was a setup," Arka said.

"We don't even know about that word," Draco reminded her. "We haven't figured out what it means." Arka nodded, accepting that this might be their only option.

"Well, maybe they'll know or at least have gotten further in figuring it out," Lumi reasoned.

Draco turned to the other three dragons. "We're in!"

Arka stepped up to the makeshift table and fixed her gaze on Raze, planting her claws on the door. "So, what's this about a revolution?"

Raze flashed a fanged grin. "It's about fixing what's been broken. It's about reclaiming our creative freedom. We need to find the missing relics and figure out this ritual to combat the attack on creativity in Draconia and save the banished designers."

Draco stood next to Arka. A frown creased his brow. "But what can we do? We're just a bunch of young dragons."

Roth pushed himself off the cracked and crumbling pillar, his voice gruff but determined. "We may be young, but we've got fire in our hearts and dreams in our souls. And with a little courage, we can move mountains. Or change the face of graphic design as we know it."

Lumi chimed in, her eyes sparkling with enthusiasm. "Yeah! We have the power to shape Draconia's future!" She looked at Roth, deflating slightly. "But... how, exactly? And what do you mean 'fixing what's been broken'?"

Raze gestured to a tattered map spread out on the makeshift table. "We have to start by finding the remaining four relics."

"Pardon me," Arka interrupted. "But... 'finding'? So, they are missing? Okay, what about the competition?"

"Draco," Lumi murmured.

"We should back up and go over everything from the beginning," Cipher said, eyes flicking to Raze before Draco could respond to Lumi. "This will be a lot of intel to take in all at once."

"Draco," Lumi said again, this time more urgently.

"What is it, Lumi?"

Lumi pointed at the map spread on the table. "Look."

Draco took a closer look at the map and was shocked to discover he recognized it. Well, obviously, he recognized it. It was a map of Draconia, his home. But it would be more accurate to say he recognized the style. It looked exactly like the map from the book, but the places were all unjumbled, and it looked correct.

Draco stared at the map, his eyes wide with a mix of wonder and confusion. The bold lines connected in a way that felt almost like they were trying to tell him something, whispering a story he couldn't quite understand. As his claw traced the edge of the map, a nagging sense of familiarity tugged at his thoughts. He'd seen something like this before. It reminded him of the Guardian, the way her voice echoed in his mind, urging him to look deeper, to see beyond the obvious. "There's something here," he whispered, more to himself than anyone else.

The lines on the map seemed to pulse with energy, as if each stroke had been made with intention by someone who truly understood the power of design. Draco's thoughts spun as he recalled the Guardian's presence—not just in her words, but in the way she seemed to breathe life into everything around her.

Draco took the book out and laid it on the table. It opened by itself, making the other three young dragons jump, and flipped quickly to the page where the map had originally been.

"The book!" breathed Cipher, reaching out a claw. "I've only heard rumors... will you let me study it?" The book buzzed angrily, and Cipher yanked back her claw. "Apologies, book. I wasn't aware you were sentient... let me make a note to stay non-invasive." She produced a notebook and scribbled something down.

The book glowed, and the places on the map rearranged themselves. It was like being near the correct map had triggered some magical transformation, and now the map in the book matched the map on the table in front of them.

"Wow," Draco breathed.

"If we could make a map as stunning as this, we would certainly win that competition," Arka said.

"Let me inquire from you three: have you ever heard of the four legendary designers Chip Kidd, Stefan Sagmeister, Paula Scher, and Gail Anderson?" Cipher asked, tapping her quill against her notebook.

Arka and Draco both shook their heads. "No, we haven't."

"Exactly," Cipher said, her eyes narrowing. "These designers are crucial members of the Design Council. The fact that you don't know their names is a direct result of the erasure. Their identities and contributions have been wiped from memory, leaving the competition shrouded in mystery. Do you mean to tell me that you three are trying to win a competition thrown by designers whose very existence you're unaware of?"

"I..." Draco's head spun. "I don't know. I feel like we learned about them in school, right? But why can't I remember any of their names?"

"Me neither," Arka murmured. "And my memory is impeccable."

Raze nodded. "Exactly. The Design Council is the one who paved the way for creativity in Draconia. But these designers—Paula Scher, Chip Kidd, Gail Anderson, and Stefan Sagmeister—are not just ordinary designers. They are human. Yes, you heard me right. They were granted the rare honor of becoming members of the Draconian Design Council for their deeds of valor in defense of our realm. Though they hail from the human lands beyond Draconia, they are the only humans who know of our realm's existence, and have vowed secrecy. Celestia's dark force banished them to a state of limbo, severing their connection to their families and lives in both the human world and Draconia, leaving their creative influence trapped and forgotten."

Cipher leaned in, her eyes gleaming with insight. "Let me tell you what I know about them. The Design Council members each had a unique philosophy. Chip Kidd was known for his striking book covers that opened the door and welcomed you into the story, instantly capturing the essence and inviting readers to step inside. Gail Anderson's work often featured rich textures and layers, creating complex visual narratives whether on the covers of books or the pages of magazines, drawing readers into the story before they even began to read."

Draco, intrigued, asked, "What about Paula Scher and Stefan Sagmeister?"

Roth continued, "Paula Scher revolutionized typography, using it to set the mood and tone of a piece, making the text itself an integral part of the design. Stefan Sagmeister, on the other hand, was a rule-breaker who believed design should evoke strong emotions and challenge conventions, often using bold and unconventional methods."

Lumi's eyes widened. "So, these designers weren't just artists; they were storytellers and innovators.

Raze nodded. "Yes, and their work influenced not just Draconia but the entire world of design. But now, their names and contributions are being erased, hidden from memory. We believe a dark force is behind this, seeking to stifle creativity and innovation."

Draco felt a chill. "And the competition?"

"We think the competition is a front, designed to distract and obscure the truth," Cipher explained. "No one has seen the Council members for weeks, yet they're supposedly running this event? It's suspicious, to say the least."

"It was right under our snouts this whole time," Arka said, echoing Draco's thoughts.

"If we can find the four Relics of Design and return them, we can unite the creative community and spark a revolution against whatever dark force is pursuing them in the first place," Roth continued.

"The erasure isn't complete," Cipher said, a note of determination in her voice. "In her rush to erase their legacy, Celestia made mistakes. Fragments of their influence—old articles, designs, and partial memories—still linger, scattered across Draconia. We, the Midnight Shadows, have painstakingly gathered these remnants, piecing together the legacy that Celestia tried to destroy. It's these fragments that keep the knowledge of designers like Stefan Sagmeister, Gail Anderson, and Chip Kidd alive, even as their physical forms are banished to a limbo realm beyond our reach."

Raze nodded in agreement. "Our mission is to guard these

fragments and make certain their legacy endures. We won't let their influence be wiped out entirely."

Draco's mind raced between excitement and fear. He could hardly believe he was now part of a conspiracy that stretched across all of Draconia. Yet, under that thrilling sensation, his rational side warned him that this might be more than he could handle.

"We've managed to secure the help of the last remaining member of the Council, Paula Scher," Cipher continued, her tone solemn. "She's the only one who has resisted Celestia's dark force. But the others—Chip Kidd, Gail Anderson, and Stefan Sagmeister—have had their identities and contributions erased from memory."

Draco and his friends exchanged stunned glances. The fact that the Midnight Shadows were working with the final surviving Council member felt almost too much to believe.

Roth, gesturing to a map on the table, added, "This is one of her maps, and so is the one in the book."

Lumi's eyes widened in realization. "That's why the book and the Guardian both pointed us to her—because she's the key to saving the rest of the Council!"

"So, let's find the Council and show them the book!" Lumi exclaimed, glancing around the warehouse.

Cipher's expression darkened as she spoke. "The three Legendary Designers went missing and we have a strong suspicion Celestia has banished them to limbo, a realm outside the protection of Draconian magic."

Raze shifted uneasily. "We should definitely head home soon. Our parents are going to start wondering where we are."

"Even revolutionaries have a curfew?" Draco asked. Raze shrugged.

"Shall we collect you three tomorrow to help us?" Cipher tapped her pen against her notebook. "Say, the crack of dawn?"

"Dawn?" Lumi squeaked. "During summer?" she asked.

"Wait, but we have work," Draco remembered. "It's our first

real day tomorrow. Don't you need us to search for something or whatever you wanted us to do at the firm?"

"You're correct," Cipher said. "I am sorry. I get all worked up when I talk about this. You can see it in my composure."

Draco stared at her face. She looked exactly the same as she had before—wide, searching eyes and a slight monotone twist to her mouth. "Uh-huh," Draco said.

"I can tell," Arka said, and it didn't sound like she was being sarcastic.

"Great," Cipher said, her voice steady. "We'll begin your preparation tomorrow. Over the next week, you'll undergo the necessary training to hone your skills. Only then will you be ready for the challenges ahead."

Arka raised a claw, a thoughtful expression crossing her face. "I appreciate the clarity on our training, but what exactly will we be doing once we're ready?"

Raze, who had been listening intently, shot a quick glance at Cipher before stepping forward. "That's something we'll discuss in detail when the time comes. For now, focus on the training."

Lumi, ever curious and quick to lighten the mood, blinked and grinned. "Does this training involve any 'how not to get singed by your own flame' lessons? Asking for a friend, obviously."

Draco and Arka exchanged glances, their uncertainty not entirely erased by Lumi's humor, but her playful attitude brought a small smile to their faces.

"We should know what we're getting into, right?" Lumi said, her usual curiosity tinged with a hint of trust.

Draco glanced over at Arka. She was usually good at hiding her emotions, but as someone who knew her well, Draco could tell she was just as suspicious and confused as he felt on the inside.

Roth hesitated, choosing his words carefully. "You won't know exactly what to look for, and that's okay. The Codex holds many secrets, and some things will only become clear when the time is right."

Arka frowned, her brow furrowing in thought. "So, we're heading into this blindly?"

Roth offered a small, reassuring smile. "Not blindly—just with a sense of trust. Your training will prepare you to recognize what's important when you encounter it. For now, focus on honing your skills."

Raze nodded in agreement, then took to the air with a powerful beat of his wings, ascending to the rafters where the last rays of the setting sun cast long shadows through the broken windows. "We'll talk more tomorrow," he called down to them. "If you're still up for the challenge, that is."

Draco looked at both of his friends, then up at the giant red dragon perched above them. "I think we are. But for now."

Roth cocked his head. "For now?

"Until you do something untrustworthy," Arka said. Lumi nodded in solemn agreement.

"That seems like a fair deal to me," Cipher said, her voice echoing slightly in the dim chamber. She lifted off and joined Raze on the rafter, Roth following close behind. "Tomorrow, after your work is done," she called down to the dragonlets. "We will begin your training. Gaining insight into the skills and philosophies of Paula Scher, Chip Kidd, Stefan Sagmeister, and Gail Anderson is crucial for the challenges you will face. Only when you have a deep understanding of their work will you be ready to retrieve the relics."

Before Draco, Lumi, or Arka could respond, the Midnight Shadows pulled their masks down over their snouts and, with a swift, practiced motion, wriggled one by one out the broken window. Like their name implied, they vanished into the night, leaving behind only the faintest whisper of wind as a reminder of their presence.

Draco let out a long breath, trying to release the tension that had been mounting in his shoulders, easing only slightly as the room returned to its usual quiet. Drama wasn't high on his priority list for the rest of the evening, so he simply shrugged and followed Lumi and Arka as they made their way up and out the same window they had entered. The promise of learning all they could about the designers stirred a deep excitement within him, but he couldn't shake the sense of unease as Celestia's name hung in the air like a lingering fog, clouding his thoughts.

The next day, Draco, Lumi, and Arka met at The Big Tree, their excitement tempered by the uncertainty of what they were about to face. They began their internship at Flametail Design, where they spent their days shadowing experienced designers, assisting with projects, and helping with research or fine-tuning designs alongside the professionals. The work was fascinating but demanding, and by the time evening rolled around, they had a new appreciation for what designers go through and were already feeling the weight of their new responsibilities.

As the sun dipped below the horizon, the trio made their way to the FlynnWare building to meet with the Midnight Shadows. The prospect of learning from these mysterious dragons was thrilling, but they couldn't shake the nagging question: could they truly trust the Midnight Shadows? And they weren't entirely sure—was Celestia really as dangerous as they had been warned?

"But it's summer break! We shouldn't be stuck studying on a beautiful summer night like this!" Lumi said as they walked together toward the FlynnWare building. She had stopped to admire the sky. It was a warm and pleasant evening indeed.

"Come on, Lumi, we don't want to be late. And besides, the Midnight Shadows offered to help us prepare, not just to learn!" said Arka, pulling Lumi with a paw.

"Prepare us for what, though?" Draco asked.

Arka paused, thinking carefully before replying, "Hmm, I'm not sure. But we're about to find out!"

They arrived at the FlynnWare building and slipped in through the same broken window as before. Once inside, the offices felt just as they had during their first visit—dark, mysterious, and filled with long shadows that stretched across the floor. The dragonlets hovered for a moment, taking in the familiar yet unsettling atmosphere, before gliding down to the floor. The open space was still scattered with large boxes, three of which had been arranged in a circle with a large board behind them. The atmosphere was eerily silent, amplifying the sense of anticipation.

"Um, hello? Cipher?" Draco called out, but heard nothing back.

There were books on top of the boxes—a space for each of the dragonlets along with another book near the large board on a makeshift desk.

"Look! It's a book about Paula Scher!" Lumi said excitedly as she picked up one of the books.

"This one is about Chip Kidd!" said Arka, moving to look at her book.

"I have Stefan Sagmeister..." Draco said, reading the title of the book near him.

Suddenly, there was a swoosh of wings around the dragonlets as Cipher, Raze, and Roth appeared near the board.

"And we have Gail Anderson's book here," Cipher said, grinning at the dragonlets. "So you have returned to us and on time too!"

"Thank you for having us, although we're still not sure what we're being prepared for," said Draco.

Roth stepped forward, holding Gail Anderson's book. "We are going to teach you about the four legendary graphic designers—about their work and the techniques you will need for the challenges ahead!"

"For challenges? But we aren't fighters!" Arka's voice was unsteady.

"Speak for yourself, I have a mean right hook..." Lumi was demonstrating in case they didn't believe her.

"The relics protected by Paula Scher, Chip Kidd, Stefan Sagmeister, and Gail Anderson, along with their life's work, have been stolen. These designers were pioneers in their fields and became key members of the Design Council in Draconia," Roth said seriously, his voice echoing in the chamber. "Each relic holds unique magic, and without them, the creative spirit of Draconia is at risk."

Draco's mind raced. "You believe Celestia is involved?"

"We suspect so," Raze replied, his tone grave. "But we don't know for sure. That's why we need you to infiltrate Flametail Design and help us recover the relics."

The dragonlets fell silent, the weight of the task ahead settling heavily on their young shoulders. They were being asked to step into a mystery that was much larger than themselves.

"Don't worry," Cipher began, her voice steady and reassuring. "This week, we're going to teach you not just about different design styles and techniques, but also how to harness their power in ways that will prepare you for the challenges ahead. You'll learn the skills and philosophies of Paula Scher, Chip Kidd, Stefan Sagmeister, and Gail Anderson. But before we start, there's something important you need to understand."

Cipher paused, her gaze serious. "As you learn about these great designers and their work, you'll also be learning about the human world—a world that, until now, has been little more than myth and legend to us Draconians. The designs these legends created weren't just for art's sake—they were made to inspire, influence, and represent people who are very different from us. Through their work, you'll begin to see and understand things about humans that none of us could have imagined before we heard the stories of these designers."

She looked at each of them, letting the weight of her words settle in. "Some of what you discover might be surprising, even unsettling. But it's crucial that you grasp this knowledge. These lessons aren't just about mastering design—they're about preparing you for what's to come, and that includes understanding the beings these designs were meant to reach."

The three friends listened intently as the Midnight Shadows outlined the week ahead. Each evening, they would learn from one of the legendary designers, gaining insights that would help them in their upcoming mission.

The first evening, Roth gathered the dragonlets and began with Gail Anderson, one of the legendary designers known for her vibrant and unexpected creations. "Gail Anderson's work teaches you that design can be playful yet powerful," Roth explained. "She had a unique way of bringing together elements from the world around her to create designs that were both captivating and meaningful."

Roth then showed them some of Anderson's work—colorful, dynamic pieces that seemed to burst with life. One example was a set of designs she created for a system of underground tunnels where humans traveled in large metal tubes. The dragonlets, who had never seen anything like it, marveled at the idea. Anderson had created posters that filled these tunnels with bold, playful typography, inviting people to engage with the art as they hurried to their destinations. "These posters were more than just decorations," Roth explained. "They were a way to bring beauty and thought into the everyday lives of humans, even in places as dark and noisy as these tunnels."

Another example Roth shared was Anderson's work on a small piece of paper called a "postage stamp." The dragonlets were surprised to learn that humans used these tiny pieces of art to send messages to one another across vast distances. Anderson had designed the illustration on a special stamp to commemorate a moment in human history where freedom was declared for many who had been oppressed. "This stamp wasn't just a picture," Roth said. "It was a symbol of hope and justice, something that carried deep meaning even in its small size."

The dragonlets were fascinated by how Anderson could make something as small as a stamp or as ordinary as a subway poster into something that resonated with so many humans. The idea that design could be a force for change, influencing how others saw the world around them, was a lesson they knew would be super important in the challenges they faced in the days to come.

The next evening, Raze took over to discuss another designer, Paula Scher. "Paula Scher's work is instantly recognizable because she wasn't afraid to push boundaries," Raze began, his voice filled with reverence. "Her designs were unlike anything we've ever seen in Draconia—bold, innovative, and full of life. She used typography in ways that made words feel alive, mixing fonts, altering spaces between letters, and playing with scale and sizing to create something entirely new."

Raze then showed them an image of Scher's work for a place where humans gathered to watch stories come to life. The dragonlets were captivated by the idea of a theater—a place where humans gathered to experience stories in a way they could only imagine. The vibrant, energetic designs that Scher had created sparked their imaginations, making them wish they could experience it for themselves. "These posters don't just announce a performance," Raze explained. "They capture the spirit of the city they were created in, a place so alive and bustling that it almost feels like a living being itself."

Raze explained how Paula Scher had designed the posters to capture the chaotic energy of the city—a place so vibrant that the dragons could only imagine it. He described how she combined different styles and influences, merging elements that were both familiar and unexpected, to create something entirely new that had impact.

The dragonlets were exhausted from the intense study, but the lessons were sinking in. The things they were learning weren't just conceptual—it was becoming part of their growing skill set.

Their training continued on the third evening as Cipher gathered the dragonlets to tell them about another legendary designer, Chip Kidd.

"Chip Kidd is a master of visual storytelling," Cipher began, her voice full of admiration. "He has a remarkable ability to take a complex story and distill it into a single, powerful image. His designs, whether for books or comics, are known for their ability to capture the imagination at just a glance."

As Cipher spoke, the dragonlets leaned in closer, captivated by the idea of an illustration that can communicate so much with so little. "In a design battle," she continued, "you'll need to find that balance between clarity and mystery—just like Kidd did with his work. Each cover tells a story, drawing your attention and making you want to know more, all with just one image."

The dragonlets were fascinated by the idea of using a single image to convey an entire narrative. The thought of being able to capture a story so completely in one glance was both exciting and daunting.

Finally, on the fourth evening of thier training, Roth introduced them to the work of Stefan Sagmeister.

"Sagmeister is known for turning design on its head," Roth explained, his tone serious yet full of respect. "He wasn't afraid to challenge the senses—whether through typography, environment, or even by creating designs that made people stop in their tracks and think differently."

Roth showed them one of Sagmeister's most memorable designs, a striking image of a headless chicken. "This design wasn't just about shock value," Roth said, "it was a powerful metaphor for the chaotic and mindless nature of work, especially when there's no clear direction. Sagmeister knew how to make design something you felt, not just something you looked at."

The dragonlets were struck by the idea of using design to provoke thought and challenge expectations. They could see how Sagmeister's approach could be crucial in a design battle, where surprising your opponent might be the key to victory.

As the week of training drew to a close, the dragonlets were both exhausted and exhilarated by everything they had learned. Each evening had brought new insights and inspiration, and now, it was time to put those lessons into practice. Cipher gathered the dragonlets and addressed them taking a more serious tone.

"Tonight marks the culmination of your training," Cipher announced. "Your final task is to create designs that reflect everything you've learned from the four legendary designers. This isn't just about showing off your skills—it's about demonstrating how you can successfully, creatively integrate their philosophies and techniques into your own work."

The Midnight Shadows stepped back and watched closely as the dragonlets huddled over their designs, working together to best determine how to bring their new skills to life.

Draco's mind buzzed with ideas, recalling the bold typography of Paula Scher, the playful creativity of Gail Anderson, the narrative clarity of Chip Kidd, and the thought-provoking concepts of Stefan Sagmeister. He knew this task was more than just an exercise; it was a test of everything they had learned that week.

The dragonlets worked tirelessly, pouring all their newly acquired knowledge into their designs. When they finally presented their work, the Midnight Shadows offered critiques that were both insightful and challenging.

Cipher praised their use of bold typography inspired by Paula Scher but urged them to push boundaries further. "Don't be afraid to take risks—unexpected choices often lead to the most powerful designs."

Roth noted their use of Gail Anderson's playful elements but suggested they inject more spontaneity. "Gail always kept a sense of fun in her work—try to embrace that more freely."

Raze commended their narrative clarity in Chip Kidd's style but reminded them to leave room for mystery. "Remember, a little intrigue can make your design even more compelling."

Finally, Roth was impressed by their efforts to challenge norms like Stefan Sagmeister, yet encouraged deeper thinking. "Sagmeister's work isn't just about shock—it's about changing perspectives. Does your design make others see things differently?"

By the end, the dragonlets had a clearer understanding of their strengths and where they could improve, realizing that mastering design was about more than just imitation—it was about applying these principles in their own unique way.

The dragonlets nodded in agreement as Cipher, Roth, and Raze's words settled over them like a heavy cloak. They were exhausted but felt ready. Armed with the knowledge of the designers—their techniques and philosophies—and how to apply these lessons in their own work, they were prepared to face the challenges ahead. But their adventure had only just begun.

It was late at night, and the dragonlets were beyond tired as they gathered their things, ready to head home. Just as they were about to leave, Roth's voice broke the silence.

"One last thing," he said, his tone unusually grave. "Remember everything you've learned this week. The relics you seek are more than mere artifacts—they are key to understanding the true history and power within Draconia. Flametail Design is not what it seems. Be on your guard, and trust in each other."

Draco felt a knot form in his stomach from this new responsibility. Of course, the fear of what lay ahead was beginning to creep in, but there was no turning back now.

"Tomorrow," Raze added, his eyes narrowing, "you will begin your mission. Celestia is cunning, and her influence runs deep. Be careful."

With those final words lingering in their minds, the dragonlets left the FlynnWare building.

The evening air was cool and still, a stark contrast to the storm of thoughts swirling in their heads. As they made their way through the streets of Everbright, each dragonlet quietly considered what the coming day might hold.

"Do you think we're ready?" Lumi asked, her voice barely above a whisper and without any of her typical humor.

"We have to be," Arka replied, her tone resolute. "Draconia has no other choice."

Draco nodded, the anxious knot in his stomach tightening. Tomorrow would mark a new phase in their internship, with a daunting new objective. They would step into Flametail Design, armed with the knowledge of the legendary designers. But deep down, Draco couldn't shake the feeling that the real challenges were only just beginning.

Chapter 14
Espionage in the Office

The next morning, Draco, Lumi, and Arka felt the weight of their new responsibilities as they arrived at Flametail Design. Their intensive training with the Midnight Shadows was complete, but they were still just interns at Flametail Design—albeit interns now with a much better understanding of the challenges they might face, and how to overcome them. Each day, they continued to shadow experienced designers, assist with projects, and fine-tune their skills, all while keeping the knowledge they had gained close to their hearts.

The lessons they had absorbed during their training echoed in their minds. The bold typography, the playful creativity, the narrative clarity, and the thought-provoking concepts—all these influences guided their actions, preparing them for the tasks ahead.

During one of their breaks, as they settled into their routine, Draco felt an unusual warmth coming from the Codex tucked away in his bag. It was a subtle sensation, almost like a soft nudge—a reminder of the lingering mysteries they were meant to uncover. Back at his workstation, Draco quietly opened the book, shielding it from prying eyes, and found that one of the pages had come alive with a swirling, spiral pattern. The design was abstract, hinting at a path leading downward, its meaning still unclear.

Draco's brow furrowed as he studied the page. The spiral felt oddly familiar, bringing to mind the warning the Midnight Shadows had given them: "Flametail Design isn't what it seems. Be on your guard."

Lumi noticed Draco's distraction and leaned over. "What's up with the Codex?" she asked in a whisper.

Draco showed her the page. "I'm not sure. It looks like it's trying to tell us something, maybe leading us to the lower floors?"

Arka glanced over and added, "The seventh floor, maybe? That's where all the old archives are. It's worth checking out."

The three exchanged determined glances, their curiosity piqued and their determination solidified by the Codex's subtle guidance. They knew the stakes were rising, but they were ready to face whatever challenges lay ahead.

One evening, while Ignisar was deeply absorbed in his own research, the three dragonlets ventured down to the seventh floor—a sprawling space that occupied the entire level. This was the domain of the Arcane Archivists, a prestigious society responsible for safeguarding Draconia's magical history. The archives were a treasure trove of knowledge, filled with towering shelves crammed with ancient scrolls, dusty tomes, and relics of forgotten magic. The Archivists, known for their dedication to preserving Draconia's rich heritage, managed this vast collection, ensuring that the wisdom of the past remained accessible to those who sought it.

As they wandered through the labyrinth of shelves, their eyes scanned rows of ancient scrolls and dusty tomes. The dragonlets began to find bits of knowledge that resonated with what they had been learning. Draco paused at a large, old book with intricate designs on the cover. Flipping through its pages, he noticed bold, eye-catching letters that seemed to jump off the page. The letters were arranged with a kind of precision that made them feel almost alive, as if they were telling a story of their own.

Lumi, ever curious, pulled out a scroll filled with bright, colorful posters from Draconia's past. The posters mixed images and words in a way that made even the simplest messages stand out. They were more than just announcements—they seemed to turn everyday communication into something exciting and memorable.

Arka pulled out another book and found a series of simple drawings, each illustrating a story with just a few strokes of ink. The designs were so clean and clear that they made a big impact without needing any extra detail. It was a great reminder that sometimes, less is more when you want to make a strong point.

Then, they stumbled upon something completely unexpected—a cryptic reference to a mysterious tome. They had come to the archives for a different purpose altogether, but this discovery went beyond their initial objective, leaving them unsure of its full significance. As they carefully studied the faded script, Arka's sharp eyes caught a subtle hint buried within the text—a reference to a hidden location.

"It's here," Arka whispered excitedly, tracing her claw along the worn parchment. "Another book, or... something. The text mentions a secure location within Flametail Design—deep inside Celestia's office."

Draco's brow furrowed with curiosity and Lumi's eyes widened in anticipation. The knowledge they had gained during their late-night sessions was crucial, but now it seemed like it was only the beginning. They had been prepared for this moment, yet the task ahead felt more daunting than ever.

After their exploration on the seventh floor, the dragonlets knew it was time to return to their internship duties. They couldn't stop thinking about the secrets they had uncovered as they ascended back to the 14th floor.

Draco noticed his father, deeply engrossed in a creative project studying various scrolls and manuscripts. Ignisar, ever watchful from his desk, let his guard slip for just a moment. His eyes flickered, and the corner of his mouth twitched as if he was holding back something he knew. Did he understand the true nature of the hidden tome, or was it just a brief crack in his usually composed demeanor?

As they gathered for their afternoon break, the three exchanged nervous glances, silently planning their next move. With determination and a spark of mischief, they decided to avoid the watchful eyes of the guards and quietly head upstairs to Celestia's office. Little did they know, the secrets they sought would unlock mysteries beyond their wildest imaginations.

Draco, Arka, and Lumi stood outside Celestia's grand office. The air crackled with anticipation as they exchanged nervous glances. They had come here with a daring mission to retrieve a magic book rumored to hold immense power. Grocklepot was away from his desk for once.

Draco took a deep breath and pushed open the heavy door.

They stepped inside cautiously, their claws clicking softly against the polished marble floor.

The office was as vast as Draco remembered, and since they were there on purpose this time, he felt he could look around a little. The space was filled with towering bookshelves and ornate tapestries depicting ancient battles. Sunlight streamed through monotone stained-glass windows, turning the natural light gray and white and casting geometric patterns across the room.

Lumi sniffed the air. "I smell it," she whispered. "I smell the scent of magic."

"You have to be joking," Draco whispered back.

"No, I'm not," Lumi insisted, slightly louder. "Sniff the book, and then smell the air in here! It literally smells the same."

Draco pulled out the Codex of Design and inhaled deeply. The only scent that tickled his nostrils was the smell of old leather. The book rattled in his claws, seemingly indignant at being sniffed. Draco would be upset, too. "Lumi," he said quietly. "I think you just smell the scent of books.""Quiet, both of you," Arka hissed, making Lumi and Draco jump in shock. "Split up and search the room. Keep an eye out for anything suspicious."

They fanned out, their eyes scanning the shelves and desks for any sign of the elusive book. Piles of paperwork littered the desks, and Draco wrinkled his nose as he sifted through stacks of parchment detailing graphic design projects.

"She has this obsession with symmetry and order," Draco muttered, tossing another brochure aside. "It's getting a bit old."

"Order, schmorder. If her office was more orderly, we'd be able to find that book," Lumi said derisively.

"Focus, guys," Arka called quietly over her shoulder.

Lumi grinned and, with a playful flick of her wing tip, performed a mock salute. "Yes, boss! On it, boss!" she chirped before spinning around on her heel, like a soldier. Marching back to work, she exaggeratedly scanned the room with one paw over her brow, as if she were an explorer on a grand safari.

Minutes ticked by as they continued their search of Ms. Celestia's office that felt like hours to the three dragonlets on their search. Each passing second made Draco feel queasy with worry. What if his dad caught them? Or worse, Ms. Celestia did? She was scary enough without finding them inside her office without permission! They needed to find this book, and they had better do it quickly!

"I think I may have found something. Could it be this?" Lumi was holding a book in her claws called The Secret Key. The book was beautiful, it was bound in black leather with gold lettering which appeared three dimensional almost, with intricate parts to each letter that joined together to make an elaborate and stunning design. The font was a swirling spidery style, with each letter formed closely together with ornate swirls and loops.

Draco moved across the room and peered over Lumi's shoulder. "I don't think this is what we need. Would it really be that easy? Let's check if it is, anyway."

He reached inside his satchel and pulled out the Codex of Design which did not react when placed near the book Lumi found. Nothing happened.

"Oh, rats' tails!" Lumi said and smoke billowed through her snout as she sighed. "Finding this book is taking forever and I'm hungry! We are supposed to eat on our lunch break, you know?" Lumi was dreaming of the spaghetti from the night before with a glazed expression on her face.

Draco tried putting the Codex of Design away in his satchel again but felt like it didn't want to go away. He was beginning to recognize the book's moods, and right now he felt something like resilience from it, a magnetic pull stopping him from putting the book away.

Just then they could hear a muffled noise in the corner of the room. A faint clinking noise.

"What was that? Was that you, Lumi?" Arka asked from near a pile of scrolls she was sifting through.

"No! Maybe it was the noise of your own dragon fire seeping out from your rear end..." Lumi teased and was laughing uncontrollably at her own joke.

"Wait, shush, I can hear it too!" Draco said, as he searched for the culprit of the sound. Was somebody coming? No, it sounded inside the office itself, more specifically within the walls in the corner of the room. The muffled glass noise could be heard if you stood very still.

But what was making it?

Draco neared the corner of the room and could feel the book vibrating in his satchel. They were doing the right thing to search out whatever the noise was, he could tell. He just hoped they could find out what it was and find this other book before anyone caught them inside the office.

There was a tapestry covering the back wall and as Draco neared it, the book was vibrating like crazy. He could hear the clink-clink noise loudest over here, too.

"It's over here, guys! Maybe it's behind this tapestry?" Draco moved the large tapestry with his claw but there were only gray bricks behind it. The stone wall was taunting them.

Lumi flew across the room, still holding The Secret Key in her claws. "Maybe there's some sort of hidden door? I can hear that clinking noise here, so it must be behind this wall."

Arka sniffed. "But there's only the wall here, see?" She ran her scales across the walls and felt nothing.

Draco stared and wondered what they were missing. The book in his satchel was still buzzing, a sign that they were in the right place—but something wasn't adding up. The Midnight Shadows had told them the book needed to find the other, that the two were meant to be together. Did the Midnight Shadows leave something out? Or was the answer right in front of them, just waiting to be discovered?

Then Draco saw it, a tiny gap in between the stone bricks. He moved closer, bringing his eye close to the wall.

"Draco, what are you doing? Kissing the wall won't help us find this book!" Lumi giggled.

"I'm not kissing the wall. There's a keyhole here. Look!" Draco pointed a claw excitedly.

Arka moved past so she could see, too. “He’s right, but where is the key for it?”

They began a new search of the office for a key this time but found nothing in the drawers, the cabinets or even inside the books that lined the walls. They were stuck again.

“What if this is the key?” Lumi said as she was still holding The Secret Key. She riffled through the pages, but it was blank inside. In frustration, Lumi tossed the book aside. The book tumbled to the ground, and as it settled, an intricate pattern on the cover shimmered, drawing Draco’s attention back to it.

Draco took the book off the floor and stared at the beautiful cover. The title, The Secret Key, was intricately engraved in gold, deeply grooved into the cover yet appearing three-dimensional at the same time. Draco could feel the book buzzing even more in his satchel. This had to be it!

He noticed the font was so unusual and wondered if a different perspective might give him some clue as to what the book he was holding actually was. Turning it upside down, Draco realized the title wasn’t just decorative—it was an ambigram. But unlike a typical ambigram, it didn’t just look the same when flipped. It revealed a different message altogether! When you look at it in one direction, the title read The Secret Key, but when flipped 180 degrees, the words morphed into You Press It.

What did it mean? The book read the title as The Secret Key one way and then upside down as You Press It.

“Look at this! The title is an ambigram!” Draco said to the others.

Arka flashed some teeth “Oh well done Draco!”

“Yes, well done Draco... But what’s an ambigram?” Lumi said with her head tilted to one side.

“It’s when an image or some text can be read one way and, by flipping it a hundred and eighty degrees, it shows something else upside down. Look, the title says—You Press It—when you flip it around!” Draco showed the others the book in both directions so they could see it themselves.

"Wow, it's so cool." Lumi breathed.

"What's it mean though? Press what?" Arka asked.

"I'm not sure," Draco said, slowly running his claw gently on the cover. He pressed all over and nothing happened. Finally, he tried pressing the word "It" itself and heard a strange clicking noise.

The three dragonlets gasped and watched the book eagerly.

Suddenly, the words on the book were melting like liquid gold being fused together. From the words The Secret Key came to form an actual golden key. It was small and somehow stood on top of the book, gleaming in the dull light of the office.

Lumi gasped with Arka in unison.

The clinking noise seemed to intensify. And the three dragonlets could hear something else—it was coming from the hall outside, footsteps getting closer and closer towards them!

Chapter 15
Misty

"Someone's coming! Should we hide?" Arka hissed.

"No, let's use the key and see what happens! We might not get another chance." Draco scrambled towards the keyhole they found on the wall. Lumi and Arka's claws skittled across the floor to reach him.

The steps outside were getting closer and closer as Draco struggled to steady his paws to hold the golden key. The three dragonlets let out nervous puffs of smoke as they heard the handle on the door being turned.

They heard a familiar voice coming towards the door. The voices seemed to have paused outside with the door as the handle moved a half-turn. They could hear Draco's dad speaking to Ms. Celestia. "Got it!" Draco had finally placed the key inside the hidden keyhole and the entire wall opened as a door with a scrape of stone against stone, just at the same time as the office door opened.

Arka, Lumi and Draco dived through. They could hear the voice of Ms. Celestia screaming outside.

Draco locked the door on the other side and they found themselves in darkness. He left the key inside the lock.

"You three will be locked in there forever!" Ms. Celestia shouted through the wall. "If you ever come out, I will hang you from the top floor of this building!" her screams continued as the three dragonlets walked through the darkness.

But it looked like, for now, they were safe.

They were in a thin, damp, and cold space. Spiders crawled next to them as a cold breeze whipped at them. "Lumi, can you help light the way?" Arka asked, her fangs chattering.

"I can't see my snout!" Lumi replied.

"So, what, light the way!" Draco said impatiently. He could feel the coldness in his claws. "Oh right, of course!" Lumi took a deep breath, focusing her mind and with Lumi's eyes closed, flames shot out violently, lighting the hallway like a blazing inferno.

"TOO MUCH!" Arka screamed as the hallway was ablaze with light. "LUMI STOP!"

"Oops! Sorry, is that better?" Lumi gradually controlled the flame, adjusting it through slowing down and controlling her breathing, like turning down the gas on a stove. She exhaled slowly, and the flame reduced to a small, steady light at the end of her snout, gently dancing in the breeze. Lumi knew that controlling her flame wasn't just about summoning it—it was about maintaining her calm, even in the face of fear.

"Thank you," Arka said as they continued to walk. Lumi was best at controlling her flames out of the three. Each dragon possessed their own special skill, and fire was Lumi's. She had learned that maintaining the flame required her full focus—every breath mattered.

They could hear the clinking noise even louder down here now as they continued walking. The walls began to slope inwards, making it harder and harder to move. The dragonlets were forced to walk in a single file line. It was claustrophobic, miserable, and scary.

"I don't want to be in front!" Lumi cried as she realized they were forced to walk one after the other.

"You're lighting the way, so it's tough, you have to." Draco growled.

Lumi huffed, causing the flame to burst up momentarily, but didn't say anything more. They must be deep inside the Flametail Design building. How long would they be walking for? What even was this place and what was it used for?

Draco hoped his dad wasn't in trouble for what they had done. They hadn't managed to find the book they were looking for, but it felt like this was the right track to be going down, as the book buzzed inside his satchel as if to confirm his thoughts.

Eventually, the floor was sloping downwards, leading to some old stone steps. The breeze was coming up from whatever was at the bottom, making the air cold. Weirdly, the clinking noise seemed to have stopped all of a sudden too.

“Guess we are going down?” Lumi said as Draco nodded behind her. They descended the steps slowly. They had to sort of jump down once the other dragon in front had made the first leap. It was slow work, and the steps seemed never ending in a dizzying spiral.

“We should have got something to eat,” Lumi said as her stomach growled loudly.

“This is much more important than filling your stomach!” Arka hissed from behind.

Lumi huffed again. Eventually, she could see something ahead of them. “There’s someone down there, I think! What do we do?”

Draco hadn’t a clue, “We’ve come all this way, we might as well keep going. Maybe they will help us?”

Lumi leaped down the final steps but crashed onto the floor below after miscalculating the drop. As her breath caught in her throat, her light went out suddenly, plunging the tunnel into darkness.

“Oof!” Lumi cried as Draco landed on her and Arka then on top of him. “Be careful!”

“You turned off the light! What did you expect from us?!” Draco snarled back, frustration clear in his voice.

Lumi, rubbing her snout, exhaled slowly, the blue flame reigniting with a steady glow. “Sorry! I lost my breath for a moment... I need to stay calm to keep the flame going.”

In the darkness, the dragonlets struggled to get back on their feet. They were fumbling around, using their claws to reach out for something to help them back up.

The clinking noise was louder down here. It echoed around the stillness.

They must be so deep down inside the Flametail Design building. Lumi clawed out at the walls, causing an avalanche of rocks that crashed down, echoing around them.

"Lumi, watch where you're going! Please, light your flame!" Arka's voice echoed from somewhere behind.

Lumi took a deep breath, focusing her thoughts as she exhaled steadily. A blue flame flared up, bright and unwavering in the darkness. "Got it!" she called back, keeping her breaths even to maintain the light.

"Thanks, Lumi," Draco said, getting to his feet.

"But it wasn't me!" Lumi squeaked, who was standing on the other side to where Draco was.

Draco searched for the source of light and saw a small jar beneath the rubble Lumi had caused. It was bright blue, with something floating around inside it.

He made his way over and inspected the jar with a sniff. The jar was making a clinking noise that sort of sounded the same as the scratches they heard.

"Ooh, it's so pretty!" Lumi said as she moved closer.

Using the jar as a makeshift lantern, they could see around them. The dragonlets found themselves in some sort of huge cavern, with rocks towering around them from above. The rocks had moss, slime and other signs of aging, so must have been formed for hundreds if not thousands of years. On one side of the cave were two giant sculptures facing each other. They were two giant dragons, that sort of looked like Celestia. They looked stern and grumpy as if they weren't happy to be there.

What even was this place?

"Where are we?" Arka said, staring at the two sculptures.

Suddenly, whatever was inside the jar was flying around madly, banging and kicking at the sides louder than ever. Draco tried to stare closely, but the brightness hurt his eyes.

"Oh my, I know what that is!" Arka cried. She moved closer to the jar. "It's a fairy!"

"I thought fairies were bigger. Are you sure it's not just a blue bottle firefly?" Lumi said.

“No, I think Arka is right. You can see its small body and wings!” Draco said.

It seemed to agree with being called a fairy as it knocked against the inside of the jar more and more, its tiny hands tapping on the glass with increasing urgency. Draco could sense its desperation but knew he couldn’t just smash the jar open; that would be far too dangerous.

He turned to Arka, who was already deep in thought. Her analytical mind quickly devised a plan. ‘Hold on,’ she said, pulling out a small, multi-tool device from her bag. ‘I can loosen the lid with this, without hurting her.’

Draco watched as Arka carefully adjusted her tool and applied it to the lid. With a quiet click, the lid began to turn. Slowly, she unscrewed it, allowing the blue light to rise from the jar, free at last.

The tiny fairy hovered in the air, a trail of shimmering blue dust floating off her delicate wings, before she spoke for the first time.

“You saved me!” the voice from the blue light breathed gently. It flew around excitedly, flying high then swooping low again. It danced in the air, looping around in great swirls in huge motions. Clearly, whatever it was, felt happy to be free.

The dragonlets giggled and watched the blue light in the air with awe.

“It’s so adorable!” Lumi said, watching closely. “I want one!”

Eventually, the blue light came back down to them.

“Thank you for freeing me.” It said to them as it floated gently in the air in front of them.

“I didn’t realize you were trapped at first. What’s your name?” Draco asked. Draco wanted to ask what the blue light was, but felt it rude.

“My name is Misty. I am a blue fairy.” Misty said, as if knowing what Draco was thinking.

“Nice to meet you. These are my friends Lumi and Arka.” Draco said as they both waved.

The blue light floated near Lumi and danced a little, releasing a fine blue dust that settled gently onto Lumi's snout.

She sneezed immediately. "Sorry," Lumi said nasally.

"How long have you been down here, Misty?" said Arka thoughtfully.

"A very long time. It's a long story," Misty said sadly, her wings fluttering downwards.

"What happened? How have you been able to stay alive trapped in a jar?" Draco asked.

"Fairies don't need food or even water to keep us alive. It's hope that does. Hope keeps us going, keeps us alight and strong. I guess my own hope was fading a little, but I knew someone would come and rescue me, which must have kept me alive. And I am forever grateful to you all for saving me! How can I ever repay you?" Misty floated up once again as she spoke. "I was trapped in here because of Celestia. She used her powers at the Council to lock away books of design and creativity. I was appointed as keeper of the Codex of Design by the Guardian, but Celestia had me caught and trapped inside a jar, then buried in this cavern. Celestia erased the four designers and claimed the relics they were entrusted to guard, dismantling the very foundations of their legacy."

At this point, all three dragonlets gasped and the book inside Draco's satchel was buzzing, as if it knew it was being spoken about.

"We have the Codex of Design with us! We had to complete a task set by the Guardian, which brought the book to us. Though the book is missing its pages..." Draco said as he reached a paw inside the satchel and retrieved the Codex of Design, which almost leaped out of his paws to be with the fairy.

Misty giggled as the book floated towards her. "How funny that Celestia tried keeping me away from the book and my rescuers have got it with them! I think I know where the pages are. She has hidden the four relics down here, too. By hiding the pages and relics, Celestia believed they would never be found, eliminating the four designers and their work forever!"

"Where are the missing pages and the relics?" Arka said excitedly.

"In here, somewhere in this cavern! I don't know where exactly, but Celestia wanted design and creativity to be lost and forgotten about down here with me. I shall help you find the missing pages and relics so we can return design and creativity back to Draconia. I hope it will restore the four legendary designers and their work too."

Lumi started searching the cavern as if the missing pages were scattered on the cavern floor. She was using her snoot, sniffing everywhere, and got overexcited when she discovered something, but it only turned out to be a beetle.

"Who created the Codex of Design in the first place?" Draco asked as they watched Lumi.

"Four legends of design, named Paula Scher, Chip Kidd, Gail Anderson and Stefan Sagmeister. Have you heard of them?" Misty asked.

"We have, but only recently. A group we met named the Midnight Shadows explained to us who they are, but they were never mentioned in any books or scrolls we learned in school. They mentioned something about an ancient ritual too." Said Arka.

The blue fairy nodded. "That's because Celestia has done a good job in not only hiding the Codex of Design pages and the four relics but also erasing the authors of the book from history entirely."

"That's so sad," Lumi said as she wandered back over to join them.

Misty agrees, "Life was so good before Celestia gained power and made all of these huge changes. Creativity and design flowed through Draconia like liquid gold, shaping ways of life for many. I am sad that not only have I been locked away all this time, but Draconia hasn't had the richness and beauty of design since Celestia took over fifteen years ago."

Suddenly, the three friends and the blue fairy could hear banging noises from above. A rhythmic thud against stone. It was getting louder and louder.

"What's that?!" Arka's voice was shaking.

"It will be Celestia and her minions trying to break through. Quick, we better move, now!" Misty floated towards the huge sculptures. "This way!"

The three friends ran over to join Misty below the sculptures. The two towering dragons were made out of dark stone, facing each other menacingly. Was it a door? But how would they open it up? Draco couldn't see a keyhole or a handle or anything for them to get through.

The banging was getting louder and louder from above them.

"Misty, how will we get through?" Lumi said with fear in her voice.

"Allow me a moment to slip through and unlock it from the other side," Misty said before the friends had chance to respond. The blue light slipped between the rocks. They were in darkness once again.

The dragonlets were frozen with fear as the banging carried on and they waited for an eternity for Misty to open the door. Lumi lit a small flame so they could see.

A crash from above exploded, putting a stop to the banging. They were through.

"Come on Misty!" Draco shouted through the door. The three had their backs to the door.

"What if she's left us? What will we do if Celestia catches us?" Arka whispered. Something was crashing down the stairs towards them, but Draco could not see what it was. Just then Lumi screamed, and the light suddenly went out.

Chapter 16
The World of Changing Covers

"Lumi!" Draco shouted. "Are you ok? What's happened?"

But Lumi did not answer as the door behind them fell open. Blue light spilled into the cavern once again and the three dragonlets fell through. A skittling sort of noise could be heard as the doors were closing behind them. Draco saw through a small gap and felt sick with what he could see. Whatever they were, they had far too many legs and were hurtling towards him fast.

The doors closed with a thud and the sounds from the cavern stopped.

"I am so sorry it took me so long to get you through, are you all ok?" Misty floated above their heads.

"Lumi! Are you all right?" Draco looked over at his friends to make sure they were both there.

"Yes. I am." She was still scared.

"Did you see the giant spiders? Is that why you screamed?" Draco whispered, and she nodded.

"Ew, spiders?" Arka was disgusted.

"Celestia has her own powers. She uses Typetangle spiders to do her bidding and dirty work." Misty said.

"What are Typetangle spiders? Are we safe in here?" Draco asked, looking around him. They were in a similar cavern to the one through the door. It was cold, dark and damp, but at least they were safe.

"We should be safe, but we should make our way through, just in case they somehow get through. Celestia's Typetangle spiders were created by magic. They have chaotic twisted bodies that resemble jumbled text on long spindly legs. Their webs are intricately patterned with chaotic tangles of letters and words. They make it impossible to understand any written material caught in their webs. They can trap individual thoughts in their web, leaving their victims incapable of thinking or communicating clearly." Misty floated ahead of them to lead the way.

Lumi shuddered. "That's horrid."

Draco gave Lumi a cuddle, and she seemed better. Arka also gave her a hug before they followed Misty. She floated ahead, in the middle of dark hallways covered in rock and stone.

"What is this place, Misty?" Arka asked as they walked.

"It's a sort of tomb, I believe. This is what Celestia created to keep the history of design and creativity a secret. I don't know exactly what's down here, but I assume we will be able to find the lost pages that belong to the Codex of Design and hopefully one of the four relics. I just don't know what's guarding them. There is ancient magic within here; I can feel it."

Draco didn't like the sound of that.

Misty picked up on his thoughts as she slowed to say, "Don't worry, dragonlets. You have me now and I won't let anything harm you. I can't deny that this won't be dangerous, but I will do everything in my power to keep you safe. I owe you my life for setting me free and we need to work together to bring back creativity and design to Draconia."

"But we are defenseless, even with you here to help us, Misty?" Lumi said quietly.

"You have the Codex of Design! Even without the pages inside, it should be able to help you when you need it most." Misty said.

The book inside Draco's satchel buzzed as if to agree. "What do you mean, Misty?"

"It will grant each of you abilities to help you on your quest. What Celestia didn't realize is that design has its own magic. By trying to erase it from history and destroying the Codex of Design, or so she thought, it created its own magical abilities. You'll see. We just need to find some of the missing pages first and maybe it might reveal something."

"But why did Celestia want the Codex and other graphic design knowledge to be hidden? Why was she so intent on erasing the designers from history?" Arka wondered.

"It's hard to explain, because I am only assuming the reasons as to why, but I believe she was jealous of the four legends of design. Many years ago, designers such as Chip Kidd, Gail Anderson, Paula Scher and Stefan Sagmeister were pioneers in graphic design and creativity. They became famous, their works revered and meanwhile Celestia's own graphic design work was being ignored. She vowed to erase their work when the Codex of Design was being written. Celestia set out to do this, using the power of an evil witchcraft to achieve erasure of the Codex but went too far. I believe she was scared of the Codex and the power it had. The Codex has powers that even I do not know of!"

They headed deeper into the cavern and darkness and didn't speak for a while as they each thought about The Codex, about Celestia and how someone could be so horrible to erase design from Draconia entirely.

It seemed to get warmer and brighter too as they walked. Misty was floating in front of the three dragonlets and the dark cavern halls opened up into a huge brightly lit room with rows and rows of different books covering the walls from floor-to-ceiling inside wooden bookcases. There must have been thousands if not millions of books of all shapes and sizes, some grubbier than others, some looked brand new in paperback, hardback and even scrolls rolled tightly together. It was a hidden and well-stocked library. But nobody was there. It was empty.

"Ooh, just look at all the books!" Arka squealed with delight. She immediately rushed over to the first bookcase nearest to her and browsed the titles with awe.

Misty floated ahead while Lumi and Draco looked around. Below his claws was a soft red carpet that was framed around the edges in gold. It looked like once it must have been expensive, but now looked faded and well used with marks and dirt covering most of the space. On the shelves, books didn't seem to be in any sort of order.

"They're all books about design." Arka said as she continued to walk along the shelves.

"This is where Celestia has gathered all the books of Draconia and locked them away from ever being seen again." said Misty.

"How are we supposed to find the missing pages of the Codex in here? There must be thousands and thousands of books!" Draco said while searching the shelves.

Then Draco noticed a large ornate hourglass standing in the middle of the room on a raised platform. How had he not seen it before? The sand was flowing downwards within the hourglass and had almost run out.

What was it measuring?

"Do you know what this is for, Misty?" Draco asked, moving closer to the hourglass. The other dragonlets also joined him as Misty floated over, flying around the hourglass as if to view it from all sides.

"I am afraid I do not know what this is. I sense powerful magic from within, but what it is for and what it does, I do not know."

Lumi got closer and closer to it, sniffing.

Springing to life, the Codex inside Draco's satchel burst out. It rose high above them and opened on its spine next to the hourglass. It flipped open and words formed within a page that was being formed before their very eyes.

"What's happening?" Arka said as they watched the book.

It seemed to be reacting to the hourglass, glowing the same shade of blue as Misty was.

A new page was forming. Different parts of the page were floating from all parts of the room and fused together to create one page printed in the book. Letters were forming on the page as if an invisible hand were writing the words in front of them. They shone in bright gold swirls and loops.

Misty read the words being written aloud, "Welcome to the World of Changing Covers. Before you are many books of design and creativity. Every hour, the books will change their covers, making it impossible to find the pages you seek. Choose correctly and you will find the hidden pages within, but choose incorrectly and you must face whatever the book has inside."

Just then, the sand in the hourglass froze. A loud clanking noise, like the grinding of cogs, echoed through the room. The screeching sound filled their ears as the shelves around them burst into motion. Books whooshed by in a blur, like traffic speeding past on a busy street. Draco watched in shock as each book's cover shifted, jumping from one volume to another, mixing everything up in a dizzying whirlwind. After what felt like an eternity, the hourglass began to turn again, slowly tipping over as the sand resumed its steady flow. The books settled into place, the chaotic movement ceasing.

With a heavy thud, an iron gate descended over the entrance they had come through, sealing them inside the World of Changing Covers.

"What just happened? Oh no, are we locked in?" Lumi asked, peering around at the bookshelves and at the iron gate behind them.

Misty glided towards the gate, emitting a blast of light against the iron bars, but nothing happened. Frustration etched across her face, she retreated slowly, her movements heavy with disappointment.

"I believe it's some sort of security spell. With the books changing covers, we will never be able to find the missing pages to the Codex and the relics if they are in here. Even if the covers didn't change, there are far too many books in here for us to check them all. It would take us forever. Now that we are locked in, we don't really have a choice," Misty said.

"Misty, what do you think the Codex means by facing what's inside the books if we get it wrong?" said Draco thoughtfully.

"Well, I believe that this world of changing covers contains traps within the books. Another security spell. Not only has Celestia hidden everything away, but she also has everything booby trapped if someone gets inside. She has us locked in here and we have no choice but to guess where the pages we need are by checking the books."

The dragonlets' eyes widened at each other.

Lumi looked worried, "Draco, what are we going to do? I don't like the sound of opening books with monsters like those Typetangle spiders falling out!" Lumi and Arka shuddered together in unison at the thought of the spiders.

Draco wasn't sure what to say to her. He didn't want to put his friends in danger, but what else could they do? They were trapped in here as far as he could tell...

"How are we going to pick the books? Is there a secret as to what we should be looking out for?" Draco asked Misty as he watched the sand in the hourglass fall.

"Maybe there is a secret or something we should be looking for. But this is all Celestia's design and magic. What if each of you chooses a book and we take it from there?"

"What do you guys think?" Draco said to the dragonlets.

Arka looked worried. "I don't know about this. Like Lumi said earlier, we are defenseless! Who knows what will be inside the books if we randomly select ones from the shelf?"

"I agree with Arka. We need to figure out what the secret is." Lumi said.

"Ok, let's split up and search the shelves. Look out for anything that stands out, or books that appear different to the others somehow. Just do not open any of them. Call us over if you find something." Draco directed the others.

The World of Changing Covers was in a rectangle, so each of the dragons split up by selecting a wall each and searching one end to the other of the bookshelves. Lumi was on the left side of the room, Arka on the right and Draco at the back. Misty helped by floating up high on the shelves all around the room.

But they weren't able to find anything. Each of the books was different in many ways already—some older than others, some bigger than others, and every single one seemed to be a different shade of color. How would they ever choose one book to open, let alone one each?

"Find anything?" Draco called from one end of the room.

"Nope," Lumi called back. "And I am still hungry, for your information!" She stomped her paw as if that would summon food.

"I haven't found anything either, Draco," Arka shouted from the right.

Misty floated down into the middle, looking at the hourglass. "I think the books are going to change again; the hourglass is almost empty!"

"Has it really been an hour already?" Draco said glumly.

Sure enough, the familiar cranking noise started, and the books began to fly around on the shelves at super speed, swapping locations and covers. After a minute or so, they stopped again, and the hourglass turned upside down to start the process once more.

"Dragonlets, come here! I think I have an idea as to what's happening. I could use a special spell to help you in the right direction, if it works," Misty said as they gathered near the hourglass.

"Why didn't you say something before?" Arka asked.

"The spell I am thinking of is very powerful. It will more than likely use up the last of my energy and may make me lose consciousness. If that happens, I need you three to focus your combined energy towards me," Misty explained, floating to each of them.

"We will, Misty, but is it dangerous? What if you don't wake up?" Draco asked, concerned.

"That's why I need your help. Your focused energy will support the spell and help me recover if I falter. It's not dangerous for you, but it will drain a lot of my strength," Misty said softly. "The spell, Illustro Librum, was inspired by Chip Kidd, who first discovered the concept that book cover illustrations should serve as an invitation to the reader. His designs were like puzzles, each offering a glimpse into the adventure within the book. Illustro Librum works in a similar way; it will help lead us to the book that holds the answers we need."

“What does Illustro Librum mean? Misty, we don’t want anything to happen to you! We’ve only just met you,” Lumi said, her voice filled with concern.

“It is Latin for ‘illustrate’ and ‘book.’ Don’t worry about me. This spell should enable you to figure out where the correct book is.” Misty flew up high before the other dragonlets had the chance to protest.

Her blue light shone in the middle of the room, high above their heads. She began to move in small circles, swooping lower and higher with each flutter of her wings that left behind blue dust that floated in the air. The dragonlets realized she was forming a circle with a design in the middle. Was this how she cast her magic?

“She is so beautiful,” Arka whispered, her eyes growing wide at the pattern Misty created.

Suddenly, the surrounding books were moving, whizzing around. Just like when the hourglass caused them to change covers, though this time, the hourglass had not caused it. There wasn’t the familiar clanking noise either. Misty’s spell must have caused the books to zoom around.

Draco watched the books in confusion. How was this going to help them? He was about to ask Misty but saw in horror as she was falling.

Chapter 17
Chip Kidd and the Puzzle of Design

Racing to catch Misty, he half flew, half sprinted to the middle of the room, his paws outstretched. He caught his tail while running and tripped over, just in time to catch the tiny blue light.

"MISTY!" Arka and Lumi said in unison and sprinted over to see Draco.

"Is she hurt?" Arka said.

Nobody asked if Draco was okay, but he was glad he managed to save Misty, who was lying motionless in his paw. Her blue light had faded, but was still there, gently pulsing. He noticed her breathing was steady and her eyelids occasionally fluttered. She looked like she was asleep.

"I believe in Misty's strength; let's focus all our energy on helping her pull through and recover." Draco said as he placed her body delicately on top of the platform near the hourglass.

"Right!" Lumi said. "What did she do, though?"

All books were still changing covers, zooming from one to another, it was hard to keep up.

The dragonlets searched the rows of books, but all Misty's spell seemed to do was mix the covers up again. How did it help them?

Arka searched high and low but felt like nothing was different about the books, other than they were now moving all the time. Misty mentioned the spell Illustro Librum was inspired by Chip Kidd, but what did it do? She stepped back a few steps and was surveying the bookshelves when she spotted something.

"Ooh, what's this?" Arka whispered to herself. She stood even further back and peered at the shelves, seeing something even more from this angle. "Guys, I have found something!"

The other two flew over and joined Arka, standing by the books, inspecting them.

"I don't see anything," Lumi said.

"Look at the middle shelf. Start with the book on the bottom left, then move up to the next shelf above it, and continue upward." Arka said with a smile.

Draco stared at the spot where Arka had said, and he saw something odd.

The books were still moving, changing covers, but Draco could see the books on the bottom shelf, the one above it, and the next one up seemed to pause for a fraction of a second and align themselves. All the patterns on the bookends formed an arrow, pointing to the book on the top right-hand side of the shelf. It was the only book on the shelf not moving!

"I can see it! Lumi, move here and pay attention to that shelf. It will stop for just a moment and tell us what you see," Draco said, moving out of the way so Lumi could get a better view.

Lumi made a noise. "Ahh! Now I see it! It's an arrow that aligns with the books, pointing to a specific book!"

The three friends were excited and flew over to the shelf.

"But wait!" Lumi said as Draco was about to fly up to retrieve the book.

Draco stopped with his green paw raised. "What is it, Lumi?"

"There are other shelves with arrows!" Lumi pointed to one end and the other.

There were three books being pointed out to them, thanks to Misty's spell.

But which was the correct one to open?

Draco, Lumi and Arka were all positioned below each of the bookshelves, poised ready to fly up and grab the books that were being shown to them.

They decided to each grab the book at the same time, wary of what would happen if they touched one of the books. The three friends were unsure which one they needed, so decided to try all three, at the same time.

"Ready Lumi, Arka?" Draco called. He was in position to spring up and grab the book they first saw being pointed out to them. Arka was on the right and Lumi was at the back.

Draco kept wishing for Misty to wake up and help them, but so far, she hadn't stirred. Maybe she should have told them something about the alignment spell. Perhaps it could be a certain pattern or arrow they needed to go to. Or something! Not three books. Draco was feeling nervous about what was inside.

"Ready!" Lumi shouted back.

"Ready too," Arka said.

"Fly!" Draco cried out and flew up at the same time as the other two dragonlets and grabbed their corresponding books simultaneously.

Lumi had a tight grip on her book with her eyes closed. Arka was holding onto hers and stared across at the others.

Nothing happened. They were all ok! Draco gave them a nod to fly back down. They each flew to the center of the room, near where Misty lay with their books.

Arka had in her paws a blue-covered, leather-bound book, with the title scratched off similarly to how they found the Codex of Design. Lumi had a dark green cover also with the title missing, and Draco held a red one, which was the same. Each one was a large, old-looking, leather-bound book with aged, dark yellow pages within the cover.

"Keep them from opening until we're ready." Draco said, eyeing the books suspiciously, as if one would burst open with spiders or something just as horrible.

"But which one should we open? I feel like there is something more to this than just opening one at random...," said Arka. She was spinning her dark green book in her paws, scrutinizing every detail.

"Yes, why would Misty cast a spell to help us find the right book, but it gives us three instead?" Lumi said, tilting her head.

But Draco did not know the answer. He stared over to where Misty lay unmoving and hoped she was all right. The force of the spell must have been so strong to render her unconscious.

"What did the Codex of Design say? Maybe it will give us a clue?" Draco said, moving closer to the platform where Misty and the book lay. The hourglass had stopped filling with sand, as if it were on pause.

"Look, there's more text that's appeared!" Arka said excitedly as she read, "Chip Kidd's design philosophy emphasizes the importance of storytelling when creating book cover illustrations. He believes that a book cover should encapsulate the spirit of the book and provoke curiosity."

"Eh?" said Lumi, head now tilted permanently, it seemed.

"That's all it says. Let's think about this carefully. We have three books with different colored covers. Misty cast a spell to find these specific books, and the Codex of Design explained how Chip Kidd's covers have storytelling and depth. Maybe we need to do something with these covers," Draco said, scanning the Codex for more information but finding nothing.

Each of the dragonlets placed their books on the platform, forming a circle as they scanned the covers for any clue. They were careful not to open the books themselves just in case, but still turned them over and over.

"But there isn't a design on the cover? It's just dyed leather..." Arka said, frustrated.

Lumi spotted it first. "Look, there's something here! In the corner!" she was jabbing a claw to point at the bottom left of her book. It looked like part of a golden symbol.

Draco and Arka peered at it and then at their own books. "There's one here too!" Draco said.

"And here!" Arka pointed to her own book.

"But what do they mean?" Lumi wondered out loud.

Draco placed each of the books together, but the small golden symbols did nothing or mean anything to him for that matter.

Misty still hadn't woken up, which made Draco feel like they urgently needed to figure out what the books were and which one to open.

After minutes of trying everything they could think of, Lumi had given up. “This isn’t working! And I am getting tired, and did I mention I’m still hungry?”

“Yes, about a billion times already! Maybe we should just open one?” Arka said, looking at the three books they piled together. It was frustrating and also enticing at the same time.

Draco sighed. Maybe they should just try it. If they encountered something horrible, maybe the Codex would help them? Misty said it would grant abilities after all. “We might have to just guess and try a book, then?

In the end, the dragonlets decided by the wise and ancient method that has been revered in history to be the most effective—eenie-meeny-miney-mo.

It had landed on the blue covered book that Arka had grabbed.

“Are you ready?” Draco said. He had decided that the two other dragons would be better off waiting in the air, in case anything happened, they could get away. Lumi was holding onto Misty, and Arka had the other two books in her paws along with the Codex of Design tucked away in a satchel. They both nodded to give the go ahead.

Draco took a shaky paw and laid the blue-covered book down on the platform near the hourglass. He grabbed the bottom of the cover and pulled up slightly.

He regretted his actions instantly as the book sprung open beyond his control.

What came out of the book was much worse than spiders...

Chapter 18
The Flood

All at once, a torrent of water gushed from the pages of the blue book, blasting poor Draco aside like a fire hydrant. He tumbled backward across the room, struggling to regain his footing as the deluge continued.

It surged out of the book, filling the room with the roar of a waterfall. The flood spread rapidly across the platform, surrounding the hourglass and rising steadily. It seemed uncontrollable, as if the room were becoming an aquarium. Slowly, the water formed a pool that splashed at Draco's tail as he eventually got to his feet.

Arka and Lumi both screamed and swooped out of the path of the rushing water. They flew towards Draco and helped him take flight.

"Thanks, guys," Draco shouted over the roar of the torrent that continued to pour out.

"Now what?" Lumi shouted as the three dragonlets had no choice but to circle the room in the air. The book continued to spew water with no signs of stopping, trapping them.

"We're missing something with the books!" Draco projected his voice over the chaos below.

"The water hasn't reached far up the platform yet; we could land and see if there's anything we can do," Arka said, pointing to the podium where the hourglass stood unmoving.

Lumi and Draco nodded and descended, with Lumi landing on the platform. They had stored the Codex of Design and gently placed Misty carefully inside Draco's satchel.

The water was creeping up the podium, while the discarded blue-covered book continued to pour out its deluge on the other side. Where was all this water coming from? Draco had no time to ponder, as the rising tide had already touched their tails.

Arka carefully laid the two book covers out, ensuring not to open them, while Lumi inspected the hourglass. It has to be the symbols on the books, Draco thought. But which ones?

The water rose higher and higher, threatening to engulf everything in its path. The shelves, once lined with precious books, were now at risk of being completely submerged. This had to be another one of Celestia's security features—not just to trap intruders in the World of Changing Covers, but to destroy the knowledge contained in these books as well.

Suddenly, Lumi grabbed the two open books and moved up the podium with them.

"Lumi, we haven't got much time. What are you doing?" Draco shouted. But Lumi ignored him and was doing something on top of the hourglass with the books.

Both Arka and Draco stared as they heard a loud double click above the din.

"We need the blue book, help me!" Lumi shouted as she flew down the platform to retrieve the blue book, which was still flooding the room.

"What did you do?" Draco asked, joining her.

"There's no time! Help me grab the book and take it up to the hourglass," Lumi shouted as her claws struggled to hold the book.

The stream of water was powerful, requiring all three dragonlets to work together to bring it to the hourglass. Several times, it slipped from their grasp and tumbled back down the platform. Eventually, the friends managed to angle the book, allowing the water to flow out without blasting them away, while they moved.

As Draco neared the top of the hourglass, he saw the other two books had been placed cover-side down in the corners, fitting into a mechanism. There was a gap for one more book.

"I don't know if this will work, with it being open, but we need to get it cover-side down to fit the gap!" Lumi directed the others as they struggled to get the book in place.

The platform was now submerged, with the cold water rising to their legs, chilling their scales. They shivered as they worked to close the cover and position the final book.

Every time they thought they had done it, the book burst open and released another powerful blast, resisting their efforts to set it in place.

It was a struggle, but they finally managed to close the book and force it into place with a decisive click. The water flow stopped immediately, leaving the dragonlets standing around the hourglass, water sloshing around their bellies. A low rumble echoed through the room as the hourglass began to shift. Slowly, it rotated on its base, the three books balanced on top. As it turned, Draco realized that the books were engaging with a hidden mechanism, sealing away the magic that had unleashed the flood. The hourglass continued to rotate, lifting upward to reveal a large, open pipe beneath.

The noise stopped abruptly, as if someone had flipped a switch.

"Well done, Lumi!" Draco said, breaking the silence.

"How did you know what to do with the books?" Arka asked, a little annoyed that she hadn't solved the puzzle herself, especially since books were her thing. She wasn't even sure if Lumi had ever read a book in her life...

"I don't know, it just came to me," Lumi began, her voice bright with excitement. "I was really hoping Misty would wake up to help us, but as I kept staring at the hourglass, I noticed these tiny symbols that matched the books we had. It made me think of something Chip Kidd once said about book covers. He described them as the introduction to the story, like the first step into a new adventure. It's like when you meet someone and they say 'hello,' setting the tone for everything that follows. So, I thought maybe these books were doing something similar, introducing us to the puzzle. I figured if I matched the symbols, it might unlock the next step. And it worked!"

Draco and Arka congratulated Lumi on her quick thinking. Any longer and the rising water would have overtaken the entire room. Pages were laid on the rim of the pipe, in a scroll. They must be the missing pages of the Codex! Arka grabbed the pages and flipped open the Codex of Design. The pages unraveled themselves and fit into the book immediately, revealing detailed information about

Chip Kidd and his amazing cover designs. Additionally, the book displayed a picture of the Compass of Composition—a hidden relic, according to the title.

"Wow!" breathed all three friends at once when they saw what they had rescued.

The relic seemed to form before their very eyes, emerging from the page. Just like the hidden key inside the book earlier, the Compass of Composition rose from the pages and stood on top of the book. It gleamed beautifully in the light, containing strange markings and writing that moved if you looked too closely. It was as if the text or symbols were hiding something. What did they mean?

"Did we just find the first relic?" Draco breathed.

Arka grabbed the Compass. "It looks like it—according to the Codex!"

She put the Compass away and the three friends waded up to what was underneath the hourglass, now a huge pipe. They peered down into nothing but darkness.

"One of us should drop down first to make sure it's safe. I'll go. Look after the Codex of Design and Misty. If you don't hear from me or if something goes wrong, you need to get out of here!" Draco said.

"We're not leaving without you," Arka insisted.

"I know we're in this together, but we don't know what's down there. We've already faced enough traps from Celestia, and we need to stop her. But none of this matters if something happens to us!" Draco said fiercely.

Lumi and Arka exchanged a look and nodded.

"Please be careful, Draco," Arka said, worry etched on her face.

"I will try. I'll let you know if it's safe. If you don't hear anything, make sure you get out of here and find help—get my dad," Draco said.

He climbed up onto what had been the top of the hourglass, but now it was a huge circular opening, gleaming in the light. Draco paused for a moment, looking back at his friends, a heavy feeling in his chest as he thought about the possibility of never seeing them again.

Just as he reached the edge, a sudden whooshing noise filled the air, and before he could say another word, Draco was sucked into the opening.

He saw the faces of his friends whizz past him in a blur as the air pulled him with such dizzying speed downwards. He didn't have a chance to claw the sides of the pipe or do anything to slow the speed at which he was being pulled.

Downwards he zoomed, faster and faster, changing direction now and then, he was jolted left and then right along connected pipes.

Just as he started to feel really sick, he felt the speed slowing and could see darkness below.

With a pop, he was flung out of the pipe and flapped his wings to slow his fall. How much of a drop below him, Draco could not see in the dark. It was hot in here and the air felt thick with moisture. He landed with a thud and felt warm stone underneath his claws.

Even though he could not see, he felt as though he had landed in another cave. He could hear a loud screeching and whirring noise, like the sound of bugs in the wild.

What was he going to do now? It was pointless trying to shout up to the others that he was ok, as there was no way they could hear him. Draco could feel movement around him as he stood still, afraid to take a step into the darkness.

He hoped his friends would find a way out and get help.

Around him, he felt movement at his claws. He was willing his eyes to adjust quickly in the darkness to see what was crawling past. They didn't seem dangerous whatever they were as they mostly avoided Draco.

Just then, a bright blue light appeared above him from the pipe. It was Misty illuminating the walls and floors around Draco, revealing black scurrying beetles covering every inch of surface that he could now see. It was like having moving wallpaper and carpet.

"Draco, you did it!" the blue fairy said floating nearer. "The Compass of Composition is safely with Arka. This is a significant step in our quest!"

"Misty! I am so glad you're ok, are the other two all right?" Draco said. He felt warmth from the glow of light, not just on his scales but also in his heart.

"They're ok, I woke up, and they told me you had come down here, so I followed. But the pipe has now closed for some reason!" Misty said, staring upwards.

Draco looked up towards the cavern ceiling and could see the pipe was now blocked. How would they get out? Or worse, how would they get a message back to Lumi and Arka?

Once again, Misty seemed to know his thoughts. "I have given Arka and Lumi one of my orbs. They will be able to communicate with us through it."

"Blazin'! Thank you so much, Misty." Draco said, impressed.

"We can use it now to let them know you're okay and I have found you." Draco nodded as Misty seemed to glow white. "Lumi, Arka are you both ok? I am with Draco; we have landed in a cavern covered in beetles!"

"Gross. Draco, can you hear us?" Lumi's voice echoed through Misty's body. As Lumi spoke, Misty began to glow brighter and shifted colors with each different voice that came through.

"I can hear you; this is so strange. I'm ok, like Misty said. Are you both still in the World of Changing Covers?" Draco asked.

"We are. When you got sucked into the pipe, we didn't know what to do. But luckily, Misty woke up and zipped through before the hourglass came back down and closed you in. She gave us her orb and told us to wait for your message," Arka's voice boomed around the cavern.

"I'm just glad you're okay. It looks like we are trapped down here, so we will explore and see if we can find a way to get you here. See if you can find another way out?" said Draco.

“Okay, we have to tell you about The Codex of Design. More pages have formed together; it’s telling us what happened to the four legendary designers!”

“What does it say?” Draco was eager to hear more.

“The Four Legendary Designers need our help.” Lumi said, reading aloud. “Celestia has banished them from our world, casting them out of the protection of Draconia and into a desolate limbo. This limbo is a void, a place devoid of colors and creativity, where everything is bleak and lifeless. They are trapped in a world of gray shadows and stillness. Without the relics and the restoration of Draconia to its former glory, they cannot return.”

“That sounds horrible!” said Draco.

“Keep going, Draco. We will let you know if the Codex tells us more.”

“Use the orb to keep in contact with us, please,” Misty said to the dragonlets.

“Okay, be careful, you two!” Lumi said.

“We are glad you’re safe, Draco. We shall let you know what we find,” Arka’s voice came through.

Misty changed back to blue, and Draco realized the connection with Lumi and Arka had stopped.

“Did you find the missing pages of the Codex of Design?” Misty asked.

Draco nodded, “We found the arrows thanks to your spell, but there were three for us to choose from and we didn’t know which one to open.”

Misty sighed. “You weren’t supposed to open any.”

“Well, you never told us, and we opened a blue covered book that filled the room with water.”

“Oh dear, can dragons swim?” Misty seemed to be joking with him.

“Hey, I can swim. I am not sure that Arka can. Or Lumi for that matter...”

“But you figured out to use the books in the hourglass? Or else you wouldn’t be down here.”

“It was actually Lumi who found it, which surprised us all! Why didn’t you tell us what to do if you knew?”

“I wanted you to discover it for yourselves. Part of Celestia’s magic keeps creativity and design concealed. To begin lifting that enchantment, you had to work together and uncover it on your own. This challenge was an important step toward restoring design to our world. You three did an absolutely amazing job!”

Draco beamed. “Thank you. We were so confused at first, but with Lumi and Arka’s help, we managed to solve it just in time!”

“Great! Let’s see what Celestia has hidden here for us,” Misty said, floating ahead.

Chapter 19
Gail Anderson's Gallery

"Misty, what are these things?" Draco asked as they walked. He peered at each one closely and could see mixtures of letters of the Latin alphabet. It was like alphabet soup, but alive and moving. It was so strange to see.

"I have never seen creatures like it. I believe they are the consequences of locking away the books on design. Using magic has a price and cannot be contained in these halls and caverns. The magic manifests if left unchecked," said Misty. "I don't think they are dangerous to us, but let's keep moving, anyway."

The dark caverns were hot and noisy with the alphabet beetle creatures. After a few minutes of walking, the cavern opened up into a grand hall. An expensive-looking chandelier hung down, covered in cobwebs as it obviously hadn't been cleaned in a long time, but was nonetheless bright.

The hall walls were covered in various colorful paintings, in different sizes but each one was in the same ornate golden frame. Draco felt soft carpet under his claws as he stepped through.

Behind them, an iron door lowered with a bang. With no other way out, they were trapped.

"Uh-oh," Draco said.

It was quiet in here, eerily quiet compared to the buzz of the caverns before.

"This is amazing!" Draco said to break the silence.

Misty floated to each painting, pausing for a few moments before moving on. The paintings were all different, but brightly colored and illuminated by spotlights, showing images such as magazine covers, pop art, paintings of the theater, and more.

"They are all works of the legendary graphic designer Gail Anderson... But she isn't a painter. It looks like someone has painted her designs. But why..." Misty continued to float around the room.

"That's strange." Draco was surprised that he could recognize quite a few of the images. He must have seen a lot of Gail Anderson's work before without realizing it.

"There are some hidden pages in this hall. I can feel it. It's a shame we do not have the Codex of Design, as it may be able to point us in the right direction to start looking..." said Misty.

"Could we ask Arka and Lumi to help us?"

"Maybe. The Codex might not react if it's not in the same room as the pages, but we could try it if we encounter any challenges. Let's take a look around first and see what we can find," Misty suggested.

Splitting up, Draco took one half of the hall and Misty took the other.

Draco was impressed with the paintings. They looked as if they had been painted using oils. It must have been magically created as they looked too good, as if the images were moving, almost. Lifelike...

He looked at one particular work of art closely. It was a huge painting showing a stage of a production. The painting fascinated Draco as he had never been to the theater before. He inched closer and closer to the painting to take in all of the detail, his snout eventually pressed against the painting itself.

But it felt strange. Like his snout was touching water. It was cold, wet and rippling...

"Huh", Draco said, stepping back. The whole painting was rippling from where he had touched it! How was that even possible?

"Misty! The paintings are made out of a strange liquid. Look!" he shouted.

The blue fairy came whooshing over with gentle speed to join Draco. "I can see. How did you know it was liquid?"

"I pressed my snout against it by accident and it felt wet and cold like water."

"Hmm. Try not to get too close. These paintings are obviously magical, and I am concerned that, like in the World of Changing

Covers, there could be dangers lurking within. Let's carry on looking and see if there is a painting that sticks out to us?"

The fairy continued her search on one side and Draco on the other. Draco enjoyed seeing the different paintings—under different circumstances he would have loved to be with his friends, seeing all the colors and images in this hall. The fact that they could be dangerous felt odd. How can something so beautiful be bad?

He soon came across something that looked different to the others. What he could see was, well, nothing. There was an empty space, a blank wall with marks of a painting that would have been placed there. Had the painting been taken?

There were paintings on the right side and left side of the blank space. Something should have been hung here, but it was gone.

Draco searched around and couldn't see if the painting had been taken down anywhere. He walked up to the space on the wall and sniffed the air, but it was no different to the air in the rest of the hall. He got closer and closer, searching the wall, and could feel the ripple near his snout like the other painting he got close to.

But there wasn't a painting there!

Or was there? Draco got so close he could feel the cold wetness once again. Suddenly, he could feel his whole body being pulled through the wall!

He screamed as he fell through, landing on wooden floors with a thud.

"Misty!" shouted Draco immediately. But the way behind him he had been pulled through was just a blank wall.

"Misty! Help me!" Draco shouted at the blank wall in front of him. What had just happened? He had been sucked into the wall and now it sealed itself shut.

Draco waited for Misty to say or do something to bring him back and several minutes passed by as he paced up and down below the wall. But nothing happened.

He looked around where he had landed, and it looked like a gallery, but unlike the hall he had just been in. The walls were painted white, spotlights hanging above on a row that snaked all the way around.

Realizing he was in a narrow hallway, but he could see corners up ahead. There were some paintings on the walls, but were more modern in style than the ones in the hall where he had been with Misty.

His claws clicked on the shiny wooden floor below as he walked. Behind him was a dead end, so he made sure to remember it on the way back. Who knew how far this hallway would go? Or what was waiting for him around the corner ahead?

Looking at the paintings that he passed, he saw a bowl of fruit in one painting in one style and then next to it a strange picture of rows of scarecrows. It was creepy.

Moving on quickly, he saw paintings of wine bottles, a gorgeous painting of a beach on a bay somewhere obviously hot. He saw paintings of dragons and one painting that looked like a cave. He didn't recognize any of the paintings.

When he turned the corner, he expected to see rows of more paintings or a bigger hall, but he found himself back in the same hallway, at the beginning.

He was in the exact same place as before—the paintings were exactly where they had been, displaying the same images he had already seen. How was that possible?

Draco ran down the hallway, passed the bowl of fruit, the weird scarecrows and wine bottles.

They were all here! It was the same, down to every spotlight above.

But how?

He ran around the corner and found himself back at the start of the same hallway again.

This was madness!

Draco felt scared. What if he was trapped in a loop forever? Walking along the rows of the same paintings over and over?

Chapter 20
The Dragon

Draco remembered that the paintings in the enormous hall had a strange liquid feel and he had passed through a wall to get here. Maybe he could go into one of the paintings to get himself back in the hall? Maybe he should try it as a last resort. Misty had said they could be dangerous, but what if he had no other choice?

He tried running fast down the hallway and round the corner several times, in case he could trick wherever he was to sending him back, but found himself back at the start every time.

Draco tried walking sideways, walking slowly and even backwards. Every time he tried something different, the outcome was the same.

He was right back at the start of the same hallway.

Feeling angry, he flew as high up as he could, burning his scales on the bright lights above, but couldn't find any other way out. The ceiling was a deep, dark black and whilst flying, he hit his head several times.

Still, he was back at the start of the same hallway.

Wondering how long he was in here for now and even how long it had been since they sneaked into Celestia's office, it felt like a lifetime ago.

Maybe his dad would realize he was missing and come and find him?

Deciding that the current approach was of no use, Draco turned his attention to the paintings. He thought about which one he should try first. Was there any danger in the paintings that showed bottles of wine? He thought the one with dragons and a cave definitely seemed dangerous. And there was no way he would try that creepy scarecrow one. No way.

He hoped Misty was okay and Arka and Lumi. Did they know he had gotten separated from Misty? She would have told them through the orb, surely?

"Oh well, let's go for the wine bottles, then." Draco said aloud. His voice echoed along the hallway, ricocheting as if the hallway hadn't heard a voice in such a long time so wanted to share it along the walls and paintings.

He did a loop of the hallway one more time just in case and then stood below the painting of wines. It had reds, whites with some glasses full, some empty too, and even grapes laid out on a white tablecloth. The painting itself was acrylic, with particular detail on the wine labels. In other circumstances, he would have liked to look at the painting in more detail, but for now, he was bracing himself to jump through.

Getting as close as he could, Draco saw the same wet ripple that he had seen when the moth passed through the painting. Should he take a little run-up and try jumping through? Or reach a paw and hoist himself in?

Before he could decide which was the better option, Draco could feel himself being sucked through the painting just as the wall before. Not again!

He landed on the other side of the painting on a carpeted floor with a slight "Oof."

Immediately, Draco could hear the roar of a fire, and it felt much warmer here than in the hallway. Around him was an immense table with a white tablecloth and wines that he had seen in the painting. He found himself in a large room with a roaring fire on one side and a grandfather clock on the other. The walls were covered in dark wood panels, giving the space a warm yet imposing atmosphere. Despite the roaring fire, the room remained quite dark. Above, the ceiling soared 25 feet high, vaulted and intricately designed, adding a sense of grandeur and making the room feel even more expansive. The high ceilings and sparse light combined to create an almost cathedral-like ambiance, accentuating the room's mysterious and imposing nature.

Walking around the room, all Draco could hear was the crackle of the fire and a tick-tick-tick coming from the grandfather clock.

Where was he now? There was an imposing statue of something he couldn't make out at the end of the room and a silver suit of armor holding a large sword on the right near the clock.

Draco approached the armor, his claws making soft taps on the stone floor. He couldn't stop staring at the armor's strangely slender shape—definitely not designed for a dragon. Intricate designs were etched into the silver metal, carvings that looked like ancient runes, but they weren't Draconian. At least, not any symbols Draco had ever seen. The suit was much smaller than anything a dragon could fit into, clearly meant for a creature more fragile, more... human.

A chill ran down Draco's spine. Ever since he was a hatchling, he had been taught that humans were nothing more than myths in Draconia, ancient stories with no real basis. But now he knew the truth—the legendary designers were human. Raze had revealed it to him, shattering everything he once believed. The realization made his heart race. Why was this armor here, hidden away in a forgotten chamber? What other connections between dragons and humans had been lost to time? And what did it mean for them now?

As he moved, he noticed on the end of the table a copy of "On Stage"—a magazine about a theater production of the show Chicago. Its bold font caught Draco's eyes.

But what really caught his eye was the statue of a dragon at the end of the room—it was crafted from countless tiny pieces. Could it be the beetle letters he had seen earlier? They were unmoving small circular shapes, hundreds of them connected to make a towering dragon design taller than Draco. It was really impressive. And a little bit scary too.

As he got closer to the dragon, its eyes seemed to narrow almost, and he realized the small shapes were actually bottlecaps, not beetles. The huge twelve-foot dragon statue had been made out of bottlecaps! Amazed, Draco could see different designs were printed on the caps themselves, but they were roughly the same size and a dark shine gleamed on the dragon. They looked like dragon scales in the low lighting. Who had made such a weirdly beautiful and creative piece like this? Someone would have to collect a lot of bottles for a collection like this.

A low growl rumbled through the room, and shadows danced along the walls. The massive Bottlecap Dragon before him shifted, its scales glinting with embedded bottlecaps. "INTRUDER," the dragon growled, its eyes glowing with a menacing light. "I AM THE GUARDIAN OF DESIGN RELICS."

"TO CLAIM THE RING OF AQUREIL, CREATED BY THE GREAT DRAGON ARTIST HERSELF, AND IMBUED WITH THE POWER TO RESTORE CREATIVITY AND TRANSFORM YOUR WORLD, YOU MUST PROVE YOUR WORTH. AQUREIL, KNOWN FOR HER BOUNDLESS ARTISTIC SPIRIT AND COMPASSIONATE HEART, CRAFTED THIS RING TO INSPIRE GREATNESS AND UNITE ALL OF DRACONIA. FACE MY TRIALS AND DEMONSTRATE YOUR SKILLS TO HONOR HER LEGACY AND UNLEASH THE RING'S IMMENSE POWER."

Draco's eyes scanned the dragon's scales, each bottlecap pulsating with the essence of different design eras. "I must try to understand these designs," he whispered, his thoughts out loud, his voice trembling.

The dragon's eyes narrowed. "EACH RELIC HOLDS A LESSON. FAIL TO GRASP ITS SIGNIFICANCE, AND YOU WILL FACE DIRE CONSEQUENCES. **YOUR FIRST TRIAL BEGINS NOW.**"

The ground beneath him shook, and flames erupted from hidden vents in the floor, forming a ring around Draco. The heat was intense, and the formidable dragon loomed over him, its presence imposing. "YOU MUST SOLVE THE PRISMATIC TRIAL TO DOUSE THE FLAMES," the dragon commanded.

Draco noticed a large, ancient device with three circular discs stacked on a central pivot in the center of the room. Each disc was divided into segments of different colors. The device was connected to a complex Rube Goldberg-style mechanism with gears, levers, and pulleys. "I need to align the discs to create harmonious color schemes," Draco said, examining the device.

The flames roared higher as the dragon watched, its eyes glowing with anticipation. "THIS DEVICE CAN EITHER SAVE YOU OR SEAL YOUR FATE," the dragon warned. "CREATE A PALETTE

THAT HARMONIZES LIGHT AND DARK, WARM AND COOL, OR FACE THE CONSEQUENCES."

Draco immediately looked around the room, noticing three towering pillars, each fitted with large spinning discs of color. The discs were divided into sections of different hues—primary, secondary, and tertiary colors. He realized that he needed to align the discs to create balanced color harmonies. He quickly tried to recall what he had learned about complementary, analogous, and split-complementary color schemes. This challenge wasn't just about survival, it was very much about design.

Draco sprinted to the first pillar, where three spinning discs, each representing different sections of the color wheel, waited. He grasped the lever attached to the pillar and started rotating the discs. The colors shifted with every turn—red opposite green, blue opposite orange, yellow opposite purple. Draco knew he needed to align complementary colors—pairs that sit opposite each other on the color wheel, like red with green—to restore balance.

He focused on the first disc, carefully rotating it until red and green were aligned directly across from each other. The flames flickered, subsiding slightly. Encouraged, Draco moved on to the second disc, repeating the process to align blue with orange. The flames receded further, giving Draco a brief moment of relief.

But he wasn't quite done. There was still the third disc remaining. Draco took a deep breath, then rotated it until yellow and purple were perfectly aligned. The room trembled as the final pair clicked into place, and the flames vanished completely, billows of smoke quickly puffed out, then dispersed from the vents below. Draco exhaled in relief as the heat dissipated around him, giving Draco a brief moment of relief.

With the flames gone, the dragon's scales shimmered, revealing intricate patterns that glowed faintly. "YOUR NEXT CHALLENGE WILL TEST YOUR KNOWLEDGE OF ART HISTORY," the dragon declared. "IDENTIFY AND USE THE PRINCIPLES OF MAJOR DESIGN MOVEMENTS TO CREATE A UNIFIED PIECE OF ART."

Draco approached a large table covered in bottles of wine,

several plates of food, art supplies, and reference materials. Grabbing a sketchbook and a small pencil from the pile, he began flipping through the pages of the books scattered across the table. His eyes caught glimpses of Art Nouveau, Bauhaus, Art Déco, and Modernism, sparking ideas in his mind.

His mind raced as he remembered his lessons. "I've got to create a piece that incorporates elements from each of these movements," Draco thought. He flipped the sketchbook open to a blank page, his claws brushing over the rough paper. He thought Bauhaus would be a good place to start—bold geometric shapes and primary colors. "I'll use these clean, structured forms as the foundation," he decided, sketching out angular lines and simple shapes.

But the design wasn't complete yet. Draco reached for the Art Nouveau references, drawn to the flowing, organic lines and intricate details that defined the style. "I'll overlay these geometric shapes with the organic elegance of Art Nouveau," he decided. With careful strokes, he added swirling vines and delicate curved patterns to his work, making sure to balance contrast and harmony as he blended the two styles seamlessly.

The dragon's gaze remained fixed on him as if to remind Draco of what was at stake. He worked quickly, combining elements from each movement, making certain to balance each historical style with the others to create a cohesive design. He chose contrasting colors of gold, red-orange, and blue-violet to enhance the interplay between the bold shapes and intricate lines, bringing the artwork to life.

As Draco stepped back to present his piece, the dragon's eyes glowed with a flicker of approval. It leaned in closer, the clanking of its bottlecaps echoing through the chamber, its massive shadow looming over the artwork. "YOU HAVE DEMONSTRATED BOTH KNOWLEDGE AND CREATIVITY," the dragon rumbled, its voice resonating in the vast space. "YOUR EFFORTS HAVE EARNED YOU THIS VICTORY." The room seemed to hold its breath as the dragon sat back, its gaze sharpening. "BUT YOUR JOURNEY IS FAR FROM OVER. THE FINAL CHALLENGE AWAITS, AND IT WILL TEST YOU LIKE NEVER BEFORE."

Finally, the dragon's voice boomed louder than before, echoing through the chamber. "YOUR FINAL CHALLENGE REQUIRES YOU TO FIND THE RING OF AQUREIL AMONG THE BOTTLECAPS," it declared. "BUT BEWARE, THE WRONG CHOICE COULD HAVE DIRE CONSEQUENCES. CHOOSE POORLY, AND THE FLAMES WILL CONSUME YOU, SEALING YOUR FATE AND LEAVING DRACONIA DEVOID OF CREATIVITY FOREVER."

Draco approached the dragon cautiously, each bottlecap on its scales shimmering with a different light. He carefully examined each bottlecap, identifying the design era and principles it represented. He saw Art déco patterns, Bauhaus geometric shapes, and intricate Art nouveau designs.

"I need to find the one that stands out," Draco thought, his eyes scanning the scales. "The one that combines elements from all these design movements."

There was a bottlecap that seemed to glow with an otherworldly light, showcasing a blend of historic and contemporary design. "This must be it," he said aloud, his voice filling with awe.

As he reached for the bottlecap, the dragon's eyes glowed fiercely. "YOU MUST PROVE YOUR WORTH BY CONTRIBUTING TO THE MOSAIC," it commanded. "SHOW YOUR CREATIVITY AND LET IT BLEND WITH THE DESIGNS OF THE PAST."

Draco eagerly approached the task, his heart pounding with anticipation. The Bottlecap Dragon, sensing his readiness, cupped its massive paws together with a metallic clap and then slowly opened them, revealing a pile of blank bottlecaps. Each cap was pristine, like a tiny canvas waiting for Draco's artistic touch. Draco quickly pulled out his portable travel paint set from his satchel, a thoughtful gift from his father. The set contained a variety of vibrant colors, more than enough to complete his work.

Draco surveyed the bottlecaps, considering how best to integrate the art movements he had learned about. He decided to blend elements of Bauhaus and Art Nouveau into his designs. He started with the Bauhaus style, selecting bold, primary colors and painting geometric shapes like triangles, circles, and squares. The simplicity and strength of the colors and shapes made the bottlecaps stand out, reflecting the minimalist ethos of Bauhaus.

Next, Draco focused on Art Nouveau, choosing soft, flowing lines and organic shapes. He painted intricate floral patterns, with vines and leaves curling across the bottlecaps. The muted, earthy tones he used contrasted beautifully with the bold Bauhaus colors, creating a delicate balance between the two styles. Draco took great care with the details, adding fine lines and subtle shading to give the designs depth and texture.

As he painted, Draco remembered his lessons on composition, spacing, and contrast. He carefully considered the placement of each element, ensuring the designs were not only visually appealing but also conveyed a sense of harmony and balance. Each bottlecap was unique, yet they all worked together to create a cohesive piece of art.

When Draco finished, he stepped back to admire his work. The Bottlecap Dragon's scales shimmered as the painted caps reflected the light, creating a mesmerizing display. The dragon's body glowed brightly, a sign of the magic they had unleashed together. Draco felt a surge of pride, knowing he had successfully blended the styles of Bauhaus and Art Nouveau into a harmonious piece.

With a final, triumphant roar, the Bottlecap Dragon erupted into a dazzling display of light. The bottlecaps, which composed the dragon from top to tail, came crashing down to the ground with a loud clattering noise. Draco watched, breathless, as the bottlecaps came together arranging themselves into a beautiful mosaic, each cap contributing to a larger, cohesive design. The intricate patterns and vibrant colors, reflecting the various art movements Draco had studied, in a stunning artwork. He stood in awe, feeling a deep sense of achievement and astonishment at the remarkable creation his art had produced.

As he examined the mosaic in front of him, Draco noticed a mysterious, shimmering glow radiating from one of the bottlecaps. His heart raced as he reached out, gently lifting the glowing bottlecap from its place in the mosaic. As he did, a brilliant light emanated from beneath it. Turning the cap over, the glow became a dazzling beam of light bursting forth, illuminating the room. In that instant, a magnificent ring materialized, nestled in the underside of the bottlecap.

The ring had a sleek, polished finish with a triple inlay design. At its center, an iridescent blue opal strip shimmered with a vibrant, otherworldly glow. Flanking the opal were two channels filled with a soft, ethereal light. Draco could feel the ring's immense power and a connection to something deeper, but he couldn't yet understand its full significance.

"YOU MAY HAVE PASSED THE TEST, BUT YOU WILL NOT LEAVE HERE ALIVE!" it bellowed, revealing Celestia's final trap. The dragon was coming for him! Thudding loudly, it stomped with a clinking noise as the bottlecaps moved and caught each other like a chain of armor. It roared again, gaining speed.

Draco jumped to life and grabbed the ring, flying upwards in the room, circling high up to the vaulted ceiling.

"I'm not here to cause you harm!" Draco tried shouting to the other dragon, but it didn't seem to hear him.

Instead, it raised its wings and soared upward, hovering above him. It raised a claw and swiped through the air. Draco ducked and dodged, moving swiftly and nimbly, much quicker than the Bottlecap Dragon could maneuver in the confined space.

This must be another security measure designed to trap him in the hallway of paintings, each hiding something dangerous inside. What could he do?

He ran back to the table with the wines and art books and searched for the painting he had come through, but all he could see was a blank wall.

The painting had vanished!

Chapter 21
The Hidden Ring of Power

"The painting had just been right there! I even made sure it was still there before I started exploring the room. Where has it gone?" Draco exclaimed in frustration. "Not again! How does this keep happening?"

He was trapped!

To make it worse, the Bottlecap Dragon had somehow swallowed flames from the open fire and was blasting them towards Draco.

He leaped into the air, narrowly avoiding the jets of fire that shot toward him. The flames scorched the wooden floor and quickly spread to the table, setting everything alight. In moments, the entire room was engulfed in flames.

The Bottlecap Dragon inhaled deeply, drawing in flames from the open fire and exhaled, releasing a fiery blast that engulfed the room. The air thickened with smoke, and the walls danced with orange and red as the fire spread rapidly across the wooden floor.

Draco was losing hope. He couldn't avoid the Bottlecap Dragon and all the flames forever.

The Bottlecap Dragon ascended once more, its body clinking as it moved with surprising agility. Draco dodged swiftly, feeling the heat of the flames close behind him. As he glanced towards the wall he had entered from, he noticed the Ring of Aqureil glowing a vivid shade of blue, casting an ethereal light that projected a mysterious image onto the stone.

Was it trying to show or tell him something?

The Bottlecap Dragon had to swerve and crashed into the grandfather clock, flames spouting all around. Bottlecaps seem to shatter and pour from the dragon. It soon got back to its feet and was using balls of flames from the fire.

The room was quickly turning into a blazing inferno, the heat scorching Draco's scales. He felt trapped, the flames licking at every corner, leaving him with no clear path to escape. Desperation clawed at him as he realized there was nowhere left to go.

"Keep going Draco!" a voice shouted from somewhere near him.

"Misty?" Draco asked.

Draco frantically searched for the blue light, but all he could see was the glow from the Ring of Aqureil. The Bottlecap Dragon charged at him with surprising speed, its massive claws poised to strike. In a desperate move, Draco lunged forward, his own claws flashing in the dim light. With a fierce cry, he met the dragon's assault head-on, his claws clashing against the creature's side, sending sparks flying in all directions. The impact echoing through the room.

"Yes!" Draco exclaimed, bottlecaps pouring out of dragon's hip, as it stumbled back a few steps.

Flames licked the sides of all the walls and now the floor was almost completely covered too.

The Bottlecap Dragon was engulfed in flames.

"Come on Draco! This way!" Misty's voice sounded again. Her voice was coming through the ring!

"Which way? There's no painting or a door or anything for me to come through!" Draco shouted as the Bottlecap Dragon was once again readying itself to launch at Draco.

The flames around the room were growing hotter, covering nearly all of the floor and walls. Draco was floating to keep out of the way, but the effort was wearing him out.

"But the painting had just been right there! He had even made sure it was still there before he started exploring the room. Where had it gone? He was trapped! Not again," Draco thought with exasperation. It seemed like every time he turned around, something crucial went missing.

Just then, cutting through the chaos, the ring flared with a brilliant light casting a ray of pink and blue towards the blank wall. Draco, curious and determined, flew over to investigate.

As Draco moved close to the wall, it rippled.

It was like before—an illusion he was able to pass through!

The Bottlecap Dragon roared and flew straight at Draco, knocking him forcefully into the rippling painting and through the illusion on the wall.

He tumbled down onto the wooden floor on the other side and heard the painting disappear behind him with a crash. The frame clattered to the floor and was empty. The Bottlecap Dragon hadn't come through with him, leaving Draco feeling worn-out but relieved.

"Draco! You're ok!" Lumi's voice called out from nearby. Draco looked around and realized he was back with his friends.

"Lumi! Arka! How did you get here?" Draco leaped to his feet; he was a little bruised but felt ok. He gave his friends a group hug and realized they were back in the endless hallway.

Misty floated next to them. "I'm sorry that I wasn't able to get you out of there sooner, Draco. Celestia's power is stronger than I ever imagined. Only when I was able to rescue Lumi and Arka something else happened. A light activated and I could see you. I could sense a power like nothing I have ever felt before."

"It's okay Misty! Don't worry about it. I found this ring, maybe this was the power you felt?" Draco said, raising the ring up for them all to see.

Misty's eyes widened in recognition. "The Ring of Aqureil! I thought it was lost forever. Draco, where did you find it?"

Draco recounted the encounter with the Bottlecap Dragon, saying, "It was hidden among the bottlecap scales of the Dragon Guardian. There was something special about it, something I could sense, but I still don't understand what it means."

Misty floated closer, her wings shimmering as she examined the ring. "This is no ordinary artifact. The legendary dragon artist, Aqureil, crafted this ring during a time when Draconia was rich with creativity and innovation. She wove the essence of her spirit on either side of the opal, infusing the ring with her boundless creativity and compassionate nature."

She continued, "The opal represents the starry night sky, a symbol of endless potential and inspiration. The ethereal light in the side channels is Aqureil's essence, her very being. This ring was designed to restore creativity and inspire greatness in those who possess it, a beacon to reignite the creative spirit within Draconia. It's a testament to her legacy, meant to bring unity and hope in times of darkness."

The dragonlets were captivated, absorbing the profound significance of the ring. Misty continued, "This ring isn't just a historical artifact; it's a powerful tool imbued with purpose. It serves as a guide, reminding us all of the potential we have to create and inspire."

The ring shone brightly in the light, emitting a subtle glimmer. Inside the ring, hidden text lay concealed, much like the markings on the Compass of Composition.

"This is one of the relics I believe Celestia did not know about! That's three relics we now have with us, well done!"

"Three? But the Compass of Composition and The Ring of Aqureil make two?" Draco said.

"Lumi and Arka found another relic, the Palette of Chromatia!" Misty said.

"Misty used the Palette of Chromatia to save us!" Lumi added excitedly. "We were in the World of Changing Covers when terrifying creatures came after us. We were really scared, flying desperately to evade them. Then, in a moment of brilliance, Misty created a portal on the ceiling, and we soared through it just in time!"

Draco glanced at his friends, their faces lit with excitement. "What exactly were those creatures?" he asked.

"They kinda looked like the Typetangle spiders but far more menacing. We didn't dare get close enough to find out," Lumi said, shuddering. "But Misty was incredible! She wielded the Palette of Chromatia with such mastery, painting a mural that seamlessly blended with our surroundings, hiding us from being seen. It was the best magic, pure and breathtaking!"

"Yeah," Arka added, her eyes wide with amazement. "It was like we were invisible. The mural shifted and changed colors, making us blend seamlessly into the landscape. The creatures couldn't find us at all."

"And while we were hidden," Lumi continued, "Misty quickly painted a portal on the ceiling. The colors swirled and shimmered, and before the creatures could figure out what was happening, we flew right through it."

Arka noticed Draco still holding the ring, turning it around thoughtfully. "Where did you find the ring, Draco?" she asked.

"In that room where I was trapped, there was a giant dragon guardian made entirely of bottlecaps," Draco began, recalling the intense moment. "I had to use every bit of my design skills to locate the ring buried deep within the guardian's bottlecap scales, making it nearly impossible to find!" A mix of wonder and tension evident in his voice. "But when I finally got hold of the ring, the guardian sprang to life, breathing fire and came right at me. Just when I thought I was done for, the ring began to glow, lighting up the path to my escape."

"We need to get going," Misty said suddenly, floating forwards.

As they continued down the endless hallway lined with paintings, Draco's eyes were drawn to one at the very end. Unlike the others, this painting wasn't hung on the wall but rather propped up on the floor. He blinked, confusion settling in. Had that painting always been there? The thought nagged at him, stirring a growing sense of unease. Something about it felt off, as though it didn't belong.

"Do you have The Codex? We still need to find the other pages and the other relics too," Draco asked.

Lumi nodded and opened the satchel. "Right here, safe and sound! Wait, guys, look at the relics!"

The friends looked inside the bag to see the two relics had somehow aligned themselves in a line. It was as if they were magnetized together, allowing Lumi to pull them apart and reassemble them easily. The inscriptions on the relics were now visible, except for the top parts.

"Look, there's space at the top for the ring!" Arka said, pointing.

Draco placed the Ring of Aqureil, and it fit perfectly with the other relics. Letters could be seen if you looked inside the bag at a certain angle.

Misty floated over the bag, covering the relics. "We need to check this later. Right now, we should get moving."

The dragonlets nodded, happy to be back together again. They followed Misty's lead, and as they got closer to the painting, Draco noticed a picture of bright purple and pink skies that were moving! Clouds were floating past, and he was sure he could feel a breeze.

The three friends looked at each other and nodded. Misty floated through first and the others followed with a leap, one after the other.

Draco, Lumi, and Arka soared through the skies of the picture and could see an enchanted land where every line and color held the potential for magic. Beside them fluttered the blue fairy, her iridescent wings casting shimmering patterns on the ground below.

As they landed on the forest floor, Misty hovered before them, her tiny face alight with excitement. "The Codex page we're searching for is hidden here," she said, her voice tinged with mystery. "But it won't be easy to find. We must understand the Rule of Thirds to uncover its location."

Draco's emerald eyes glinted with curiosity. "The Rule of Thirds? What's that?"

Misty conjured a small, glowing square in the air with a flick of her wrist. The square divided into nine equal parts, with two equally spaced horizontal lines and two equally spaced vertical lines, like a game of tik-tac-toe. "This is the Rule of Thirds grid," she explained. "It's a fundamental principle in design and composition."

Lumi, the smallest of the dragons, leaned closer. "How does it work?"

"The Rule of Thirds helps create balanced and engaging

compositions," Misty continued. "By placing your focal points along these lines or at their intersections, you make your designs more interesting and pleasing to the eye."

Arka tilted her head. "So, it's about balance?"

"Precisely," Misty replied. "Think of a photograph. If you place the main subject right in the center, it can feel static and dull. But if you align it with the lines or the intersections, it comes to life."

Draco scratched his chin thoughtfully. "I think I get it. But how does this help us find the Codex page?"

Misty smiled. "the Codex page is hidden within a magical artwork here in the grove. It uses the Rule of Thirds. We need to find the painting and understand its composition to unlock the page."

They began their search, moving through the lush greenery of the grove. Flowers of every color imaginable surrounded them, creating a living tapestry. As they walked, Misty gave more examples of the Rule of Thirds in action.

"Imagine a landscape," she said. "You place the horizon along the lower or upper third line instead of the center. It makes the scene more dynamic."

Lumi flapped her wings eagerly. "I want to try that in my next drawing!"

After a while, they came upon a clearing with a grand, ancient oak tree at its center. Hanging from one of its mighty branches was a large canvas. The painting depicted a serene lake at sunset, with the horizon line perfectly aligned with the lower third of the canvas. A majestic dragon soared above the lake, its body crossing the intersections of the upper third of the grid.

"This is it," Misty whispered. "Now, look closely at where the dragon intersects the lines."

Draco, Lumi, and Arka scrutinized the painting. At each intersection point where the dragon's body crossed, a small, shimmering rune appeared. Draco reached out and touched one of the runes, and it glowed brighter.

"We need to activate them all at once," Lumi suggested.

The three dragonlets positioned themselves around the painting and, on Misty's count, touched each rune simultaneously. The painting shimmered, and the canvas rippled as if made of water. Slowly, a hidden compartment opened at the base of the oak tree, revealing a golden page adorned with intricate designs.

Draco carefully picked up the page. "This is it! The Rule of Thirds page from the Codex of Design!"

Misty clapped her tiny hands in delight. "Well done, everyone! You've not only found the page, but also learned a crucial principle of design."

As the dragonlets celebrated their success, Draco held up the page, its golden glow reflecting in their eyes. "One step closer to mastering graphic design," he said with a grin. "Onward to the next page!"

With renewed determination, the young dragons and their fairy friend continued their journey, ready to uncover more secrets of the Codex of Design and become true masters of their craft.

Misty had created a new portal from this world, and it hung in the air, glowing a pink and purple light.

"After you," Draco said.

The four friends went through the portal into a new world. What waited for them on the other side?

Chapter 22
Stefan Sagmeister and the Edge of Design

"Where are we now, Misty?" Lumi asked as they entered the portal. It disappeared behind them with a fizz. There was a loud, swirling storm around them.

Misty floated ahead and shouted over the roar, "Something has gone wrong with this world! I don't know what it is, but we need to be careful!"

This world felt different from the others; it instantly put the three friends on edge. The sky above was a swirling tapestry of colors, with clouds changing from deep indigo to vibrant magenta, moving in a rhythm that felt almost alive. Lightning flashed and danced across the sky, illuminating twisted trees and jagged rocks that cast eerie, elongated shadows on the ground. The landscape seemed to flow and change with every blink, as if they were walking through a living painting.

Rain poured down in all directions, soaking Draco to his scales. It was miserable, cold, and very wet. The ground beneath their claws was soft and yielding, like a bed of moss, but in shades of neon green and blue. It felt as though they were treading on the very fabric of a dream. The air was thick with the scent of blooming wildflowers, yet there was an otherworldly sweetness to it. Every breath they took seemed to fill them with a sense of wonder and unease in this magical place.

Draco glanced down and saw the massive gray clouds beneath him. How could they be walking on clouds like this?

"I don't like this," Arka said, peering around her. Her teeth chattered.

"Don't worry, Arka. I will protect you. This world supposedly holds the works of Stefan Sagmeister and the last relic. It should have the final pages of the Codex that we need. I wasn't aware it would be like this, though. We just need a bit of help while we gather our thoughts."

Misty cast a delicate charm, her blue wings shimmering with a gentle glow. The magic flowed from her fingertips, forming a protective bubble around the puzzled dragonlets. Instantly, the raging storm outside was silenced, and the cold, wet chill was replaced with a calm, soothing warmth.

"Wow, this is so cool!" Lumi said excitedly, bounding over to the walls of the bubble. It was dry and quiet compared to the raging weather outside.

"Thank you, Misty!" Arka said, shaking off the wet.

"Who is Stefan Sagmeister?" Draco asked as he dried.

Misty fluttered around, her blue wings casting a soft glow as she spoke to the dragonlets. "Ah, Stefan Sagmeister is quite the character. Stefan is known for shaking things up in the design world. He doesn't just follow the rules; he bends them, twists them, and sometimes tosses them out entirely! His designs are bold and never what you'd expect, often stirring up a mix of emotions. It's like he has a magic touch for making people stop and really think about what they're seeing. Stefan's ideas always challenged the Design Council to see things from new perspectives, pushing the boundaries of what everyone thinks is possible."

The three friends exchanged glances, grateful for Misty's magic that kept them dry. Moving freely within the protective bubble, they ventured deeper into the stormy realm. The wind howled around them, but inside the bubble, it was calm. Suddenly, they spotted a giant sketchbook suspended in the air before them, appearing out of nowhere.

"Wow! Now that's what I call a sketchbook!" Lumi exclaimed, a playful grin spreading across her face.

The sketchbook was atop a circular platform and seemed to have a similar charm around it as Misty's bubble, as it was dry. It opened on its own as they neared. It flicked open to the first page, which was filled with Sagmeister's iconic handwritten notes and sketches, each one brimming with personality and insight. In the center of the page was a riddle:

"Where shadows fade and dreams ignite,
Ascend to the place where stars burn bright.
Shape the mundane into the divine,
And the secrets of The Codex shall align."

"Looks like this is our first clue," Arka said, examining the sketchbook closely.

Misty fluttered around it, her tiny hands tracing the elegant script. "We need to find something ordinary and make it extraordinary."

As they moved deeper into this dreamlike environment, they stumbled upon a series of objects that seemed out of place—an old chair, a blank canvas, a plain stone. Each item radiated a strange energy, as if challenging the dragonlets to awaken their inner creativity. This was not just a place to explore; it was a vast expanse awaiting their creativity, a world eager to be reshaped by their imagination.

"I think these are the materials we need," Lumi said, her claws itching to create.

Draco nodded. "We need to transform them using Sagmeister's principles of design. Think bold, think unconventional," as he looked through the giant sketchbook for help.

They set to work, each bringing their unique skills to the task.

Lumi, with her keen eye for detail, pulled out her set of enchanted pastels and a fine-tipped brush. She sketched intricate patterns on the canvas, turning it into a dynamic piece of art that seemed to leap off the fabric. The colors mixed and danced, guided by Lumi's deft paw, as if the pastels themselves were imbued with a magical essence that brought her visions to life.

Arka, ever precise and methodical, reached into her tool belt and extracted a set of tiny, intricate tools. With her precision and technical prowess, she carefully disassembled the plain chair and began reassembling it, piece by piece. She used a miniaturized welder to fuse metal joints seamlessly and a fine chisel to carve delicate designs into the wood. The chair transformed into a striking piece of modern sculpture, its form both functional and artistic, each element meticulously crafted to enhance its beauty.

Draco, tapping into his natural abilities, used his fiery breath to etch designs into the stone. His flames, controlled and precise, carved elegant patterns into the rock, creating a piece that blended nature and creativity seamlessly. The stone glowed faintly from the heat; the designs standing out in stark relief against its cool surface.

Misty tried helping, but could feel a power from the three friends as they worked individually and together to create something unique, something beautiful. It was as if their combined creativity was a force of its own, harmonizing with the surreal landscape around them.

As the three friends worked, the surrounding landscape responded, glowing brighter with each completed piece. The once turbulent storms ceased altogether. The world was no longer unsettled and stormy; it had pink skies around them, like a gorgeous sunset. The ground beneath their feet was covered in white fluffy clouds, and they could see for miles in every direction as the air cleared.

Suddenly, the ground beneath them trembled, and a hidden pedestal rose from the earth. Atop it lay a scroll, glowing with a soft, golden light. Next to it, a quill shimmered invitingly.

"Did we do it?" Lumi asked, unsure.

"Are these the last pages we need for the Codex of Design?" Arka said.

But the others didn't have a chance to answer, as there came a loud cracking noise, like glass being shattered. It cracked, it creaked, and it created a deafening boom around the three friends and fairy.

All around them, the pink and purple skies were breaking up. The ground below their feet was rumbling and shaking.

"What's happening, Misty?" Draco shouted over the roar of noise.

Before Misty could speak, the sky tore open, revealing a gaping void.

From it, Typetangle spiders flooded in swarms, filling the world. The skies turned from bright pinks and purples to darkness, as clouds of spider legs blocked out any light.

"They're here. I tried everything to stop them... I am so sorry!" Misty said, sadly.

Around the three friends, the spiders were closing in.

They were trapped.

Chapter 23
The Battle of Design

The fragmented world hung in a delicate balance; shimmering shards suspended in the void. Draco, Arka, Lumi, and Misty stood on the edge of the shattered landscape, each dragon clutching their tools of creativity and design. Draco wore the Ring of Aqureil, Lumi wielded the Palette of Chromatia, and Arka gripped the Compass of Composition. The remnants of the Codex of Design fluttered on the platform, elusive and incomplete.

They stood back-to-back as the Typetangle spiders, minions of the vile Celestia, swarmed closer, their web-like threads threatening to entangle the dragons. The friends had faced challenges before, but this was unlike anything they had known. The Codex's final pages were their only hope to bring light and inspiration back to Draconia.

"She's close," Misty whispered, her blue wings glimmering in the dim light. "We must hurry."

"Remember what we've learned," Draco urged, his eyes glowing with determination. "The Rule of Thirds, the Golden Ratio, the relics, the designers... everything."

The air crackled with tension as Celestia emerged from the shadows, her presence dark and foreboding. Her eyes gleamed with malice as she approached the dragons, the last pages of the Codex clutched in her talons. Draco stared at the platform where the pages and quill were, but they were gone. How had she gotten them?

"You think you can defeat me with mere design principles?" Celestia mocked, her voice dripping with contempt. "Your skills are nothing compared to my power."

Draco stepped forward, raising his voice to rally his friends. "We'll see about that. Arka, Lumi, Misty—it's time to use everything we've learned."

Misty fluttered in front of the group, her ethereal blue light casting a calm glow. "Don't be afraid," she said, her voice soothing yet firm. "It is time! Open the Codex of Design. It holds more than knowledge; it's time to unlock your true potential. Trust in what you've learned, and let the ancient wisdom within the book awaken the power that lies within you."

Lumi quickly grabbed the satchel, and before she could fully open it, the Codex of Design floated out, its pages glowing brightly. Light energy poured outward, surging into each of the three friends, power flowing through their scales. The connection they felt to the principles they had learned was palpable, like a current of inspiration and determination.

Celestia stood watching, laughing.

In that moment, a deep understanding dawned on them. Instinctively the three friends knew exactly what needed to be done.

Arka, inspired by the uncompromising courage of Paula Scher's bold design and the striking impact of Chip Kidd's powerful visuals, took control of the environment. She used the Compass of Composition to reshape the landscape, changing the chaotic fragments into a harmonious grid, carefully and perfectly arranging each piece. The Compass became a conduit for her innate precision, drawing lines of light that shaped the landscape with exactness. Inspired by Kidd's emphasis on storytelling through design, Arka integrated dynamic barriers and leading lines of energy. These barriers repelled incoming threats, while the leading lines created clear, protected pathways, guiding them safely toward Celestia and the final pages of the Codex. These carefully crafted paths provided the crucial advantage they needed, giving them a chance to advance and reclaim the Codex of Design.

Lumi, drawing inspiration from both Stefan Sagmeister's experimental approach and Gail Anderson's bold use of color and composition, embraced the fluidity of the broken landscape. With the Palette of Chromatia, she drew vibrant colors from the surroundings, weaving them into intricate, living patterns. These patterns danced in the air, forming ethereal shapes that shifted and flowed with her every gesture. Guided by the Golden Ratio, she transformed the bleak, broken surroundings into a vibrant tapestry, her designs creating illusions and protective barriers that dazzled and confused their enemies.

But Celestia was prepared. She wielded the Codex pages to conjure chaotic designs, disrupting the dragons' use of the Rule of Thirds and the Golden Ratio. Her creations were dark and twisted, painted in muddy, soulless grays and blacks. She reshaped the landscape with unsettling, asymmetrical forms, making everyone and everything feel off-balance and out of sync. The ground trembled as these disorienting shapes emerged, amplifying the sense of unease. Despite their combined efforts, Celestia's power seemed overwhelming. The Typetangle spiders continued to hinder their progress, and the dragons were visibly weakening.

In that moment, just as despair began to creep in, Draco felt a surge from the Ring of Aqureil, which he'd forgotten he was wearing. A powerful light erupted from Draco's ring, now shining like a beacon. Draco held up his arm and watched as the Ring amplified Arka and Lumi's designs, merging their individual strengths into a powerful wave of creativity and unity.

Drawing on his innate ability with typography, Draco channeled the ring's energy, constructing powerful, luminous letters in the air. The words he was creating, imbued with magic, shimmered with an intensity that captivated the Typetangle spiders. As Draco formed commands, the letters pulsed with authority, forcing the spiders to heed his will. He directed them to turn against Celestia, using their web-like threads to entangle her chaotic designs.

Draco's role had evolved beyond only creating visual designs; he now took control and orchestrated the battle, guiding his team's efforts to outmaneuver Celestia. By leveraging his skills and the power of the ring, Draco turned the tide, using the Typetangle spiders as allies rather than adversaries. The spiders, under Draco's command, wove a network of glowing webs that disrupted Celestia's attacks and weakened her hold on the battlefield.

Empowered by the ring and all they had learned from the great designers, Draco, Arka, and Lumi poured all their creativity into one final push. Their designs intertwined, integrating the principles of the Rule of Thirds, the Golden Ratio, and the styles of Scher, Sagmeister, Kidd, and Anderson. The final pages of the Codex shimmered and solidified, coming free from Celestia's grasp.

Like their powers, the intensity of their efforts had multiplied. Their creative abilities formed a protective shield around them. Celestia, seeing the tide turning, doubled her attacks, watching in frustration and desperation as Misty flew around the friends in a circle of light, embodying unity and the ultimate power of friendship.

Draco called out, "Follow my lead!" The three young dragons, drawing upon their collective strengths, joined together as Draco began crafting a giant, unified message in the air. With Arka's precision, Lumi's vibrant colors, and Draco's dynamic typography, they projected a glowing phrase: "CREATIVITY IS OUR LEGACY."

The message pulsed with energy, resonating through the battlefield. Typetangle spiders, drawn to its bright, cohesive power, hesitated in their attacks. The radiant glow repelled the dark webs spun by the spiders, breaking apart their threads and nullifying the chaotic influence.

The glowing message formed a barrier of protective light around the dragons, shielding them from Celestia's frenzied attacks. The young dragons took this opportunity to regroup and gather their strength, using the brief respite to refocus their energies. In that moment, they realized the true strength of their creativity and unity, shifting the momentum of the battle in their favor.

Despite their combined efforts, Celestia's power seemed insurmountable. The Typetangle spiders continued to get in their way, and the dragons were becoming visibly worn down. Celestia cackled, bombarding them with nonsensical images and discordant sounds, further disorienting the dragons and testing their concentration and creativity under pressure.

Grocklepot, ever loyal to Celestia, skulked around the edges of the battlefield, staying just out of harm's way. He made many attempts to disrupt the dragonlets' efforts by casting spells and weaving illusions, hoping to distract and disorient them. As usual, his attempts at magic were clumsy and ineffective, overshadowed by the dragons' powerful unity and the protective light they had conjured. His presence was nothing more than a minor annoyance, easily countered by their focus and determination.

Meanwhile, Celestia, seething with rage, needed to regain control of the battlefield. She observed the dragons, searching for a moment of weakness. Her eyes locked onto Lumi, who was deeply engrossed in enhancing their protective barrier.

Sensing an opportunity, Celestia manipulated the chaotic landscape she'd created. She twisted the ground beneath Lumi, causing it to shift and buckle. The sudden movement startled Lumi, momentarily breaking her concentration. In that brief lapse, Celestia lunged forward, using the dark, swirling shadows to cloak her approach. The chaotic patterns she had woven intensified, obscuring her movements and confusing the dragons.

Celestia's rapid advance caught the dragons off guard. As she closed in on Lumi, the protective light maintaining the barrier and fending off the Typetangle spiders began to flicker under the strain. The moment of vulnerability was all Celestia needed. She reached out, her claws extended, ready to strike at Lumi. The young dragon, sensing the danger, turned just in time to see Celestia's dark form looming over her.

Draco and Arka shouted in alarm, but they were momentarily pinned down by a renewed surge of attacks from Grocklepot and the Typetangle spiders. Celestia's sneer was filled with triumph as she prepared to unleash a devastating blow.

As Celestia moved closer to Lumi, ready to strike, a brilliant beam of light shot into the sky from Draco's claw. The Ring of Aqureil blazed once again, tearing a hole in the sky that rippled like the portal Misty had created. A deafening roar echoed across the battlefield. "It's my dad!" Draco exclaimed as Ignisar, the mighty dragon, emerged from the swirling shadows in the clouds. His arrival was a beacon of hope, and with a single, powerful roar, he unleashed a torrent of flames that scattered the Typetangle spiders and carved a path through the chaos.

Ignisar swooped down with breathtaking speed, positioning himself between Celestia and Lumi just as the dark queen lunged.

His imposing presence and the fierce glow in his eyes brought Celestia's advance to a halt. Ignisar's flames surged, creating a protective barrier that forced Celestia back and shielded Lumi from harm. "Not today, Celestia," Ignisar growled, his voice brimming with unyielding resolve. "As long as I stand, you will not lay a claw on them."

Empowered by Ignisar's words, the young dragons and Misty renewed their efforts. They drew upon the teachings, blending boldness with elegance, and infused their designs with a newfound sense of purpose.

Just then, the Midnight Shadows arrived, descending from the clouds like a triumphant storm, their dark forms streaking through the sky. Led by Cipher, with Raze and Roth at her side, they swooped down from above, emerging from the very portal Ignisar had just opened. "Sorry we're late," Cipher called out, her voice echoing with authority and confidence. As they landed, the ground beneath them shimmered with an otherworldly glow, casting dramatic shadows across the battlefield.

Cipher unleashed her powers of illusion, transforming the battlefield into a swirling vortex of mesmerizing patterns, disorienting the Typetangle spiders. Raze, with his mastery over typography, carved powerful words into the air that crackled with energy, striking the spiders with explosive force. Roth, harnessing his sculpting abilities, summoned pillars of stone and metal from the ground, creating a fortress-like defense that trapped and isolated the remaining spiders. The Midnight Shadows' entrance and their impressive display of creative powers reinvigorated the dragons, turning the battle's tide.

Celestia, floating above, desperately tried to use her kinetic art techniques, creating constantly shifting designs that were difficult to pin down and understand. "You will not win! My designs are the only true expression for Draconia and all of the worlds that I've created!" Celestia cried in desperation, but her power was failing.

"True power lies not in control, but in the freedom of creativity and the beauty of design," Ignisar declared, his wings spread wide as he shielded the dragons from Celestia's final, desperate attacks.

"Your tyranny ends here, Celestia!"

Draco, Arka, Lumi, and Misty combined their strengths, their designs intertwining in a harmonious symphony. As their creativity flowed together, the final missing pages of the Codex of Design began to glow, resonating with the energy of their unity. The pages shimmered with an ethereal light and slipped out of Celestia's grasp, gravitating towards the Codex, which floated before the dragons. The book eagerly absorbed the pages, each one snapping into place as if it had always belonged there.

With a triumphant cry, Draco seized the now completed Codex. As he did, a surge of power radiated from the book, spreading throughout the shattered realm. The energy of the fully restored Codex flowed through the land, healing the fractures and restoring the world to its vibrant, cohesive state. The once-broken pieces of the realm reunited, forming a beautiful and harmonious whole.

In that moment, the Codex of Design, now complete and working in conjunction with the power of Aqureil's ring and the other relics, along with the combined design abilities of Misty and the dragons, unleashed a powerful wave of energy. The force surged forward, striking Celestia and instantly knocking her down, shattering her dark influence. The dragons' triumph was clear as the Codex, now fully restored, served as a beacon of creativity and unity, banishing the darkness that had plagued Draconia.

All the Typetangle spiders were now gone. Celestia, defeated and powerless, had her reign of darkness ended. As the light of design and creativity spread across the realm, a ripple of energy surged through the portal, connecting back to Draconia.

In Draconia, the once dimmed and oppressed city of Everbright began to shine brighter than ever. The colors of the dragons' creations became more vibrant, and the air buzzed with renewed inspiration and creativity.

Ignisar turned to his son and his friends. "You have done well. Today, you have proven that true power lies not in force, but in the strength of your creativity and the bonds you share. Your victory here has restored balance and unleashed a new wave of creativity across Draconia. The dark clouds that once loomed over our home have lifted, and a new era of artistic brilliance has begun."

The friends hugged each other, smiling with the realization that they had done it! They had worked together, using their skills in design to stop Celestia. She was gone!

"You were both incredible!" Draco said, his voice thick with emotion, tears brimming in his eyes.

"You too!" Arka replied, her voice filled with pride.

For once, Lumi was speechless, her usual wit replaced by awe.

As they stood together, Draco noticed something extraordinary—they were each holding a relic of design. The Ring of Aqureil gleamed on Draco's finger, while Arka gripped the Compass of Composition tightly, and Lumi held the Palette of Chromatia close to her chest.

Suddenly, the relics pulsed with energy, trembling in their hands. The dragonlets exchanged astonished looks as the relics, guided by an unseen force, lifted out of their grasp and into the air. They hovered between them, glowing brighter and brighter, until, with a flash of light, they began to come together.

The merging relics spun in the air, a whirlwind of color and light, drawing gasps from the dragonlets. As they combined into a single, brilliant object, a cascade of bright white text appeared, glowing with a radiant energy that illuminated their faces.

There was a power between them, an undeniable connection that pulsed in their very veins. They had conquered Celestia, reclaimed the relics, and restored design and creativity to their world. The moment was so powerful, so profound, that it left them speechless, their hearts too full to form words.

Misty, who had been hovering nearby, floated closer, her eyes wide with wonder as she read the glowing text aloud:

"Designers of old, who paved the path for you,
Restore their glory, make their legacy true.
With relics united, the darkness is torn,
Through wisdom and courage, a new dawn is born."

Chapter 24
The Dragon's Guide to Graphic Design

The relics continued to spin above the dragonlets, a whirlwind of color and light swirling in the air. The energy between them crackled with intensity, filling the space with a powerful hum. As the relics merged into a single, brilliant object, the light grew even brighter, casting long shadows across the battlefield.

Then, with a sudden flash, the light shot upward, piercing the sky. The clouds parted, revealing a vibrant aurora that danced across the heavens, alive with colors that shimmered and shifted. The relics, now fused together, hovered above the dragonlets, radiating an energy that pulsed with the very essence of design and creativity.

From within the heart of the aurora, a beam of light descended, slowly lowering to the ground before the dragonlets. As the light touched the earth, three figures began to take shape. The dragonlets watched in awe as the forms of Chip Kidd, Gail Anderson, and Stefan Sagmeister materialized before their eyes. The legendary designers, once lost to a dark limbo, now stood restored, their expressions filled with a mix of relief and gratitude.

Each designer, exhausted from their ordeal, was welcomed back to Draconia with open arms. Temporarily brought to Draconia to convey their gratitude, they stood before the dragonlets and offered words of thanks.

"Your bravery and creativity have saved us," said Chip Kidd, his voice resonating with gratitude. "You have restored not just our freedom, but the spirit of design in Draconia."

"We owe you a debt of gratitude," said Gail Anderson, her eyes reflecting deep appreciation. "Your actions have reignited the spark of creativity in this land. We are honored to be part of your legacy."

"You have shown us the true power of unity and creativity," added Stefan Sagmeister, his voice filled with emotion. "Thank you for bringing us back and preserving the essence of design."

The dragonlets beamed with pride as the designers continued to express their thanks. After their heartfelt speeches, the designers were transported back to their homes in the human lands, safe and sound.

In the aftermath of the battle, the Draconian Council of Elders convened to decide the fate of Celestia and Grocklepot. The charges against them were severe—betraying the core values of creativity and design that Draconia holds so dear. Not only had they obscured the legendary Relics of Design and attempted to erase the realm's artistic legacy, but their crimes ran much deeper.

Celestia and Grocklepot had used their evil powers to cruelly banish the legendary human designers to a state of limbo, tearing them away from their lives and loved ones in the human lands outside Draconia. This callous act left the human world without their creative influence that had long shaped its history. The designers, once the lifeblood of art and innovation, were cast into oblivion, their legacy erased, and their lives torn apart.

The Draconian legal system, renowned for its fairness and dedication to preserving creativity, deemed any threat to the realm's artistic integrity deserving of serious consequences. Now, faced with the full extent of their actions, Celestia and Grocklepot would have to answer for the darkness they had brought to Draconia and beyond.

Several weeks had passed since Celestia's power was diminished by the three dragonlets and Misty. They had returned to Draconia triumphantly, the completed Codex of Design in their paws. Celestia, now banished from Draconia, was transported to a world devoid of design and color—a dull void where inspiration could never thrive.

The Codex of Design was safely returned to the library where their journey began, and with the help of the Midnight Shadows, the records of Paula Scher, Chip Kidd, Gail Anderson, and Stefan Sagmeister were restored to the realms. The three known Relics of Design—the Compass of Composition, the Palette of Chromatia, and the Ring of Aqureil—were recovered and secured, ensuring the preservation of Draconia's creative heritage. The whereabouts of the final relic, the Quill of Typographus, remained unknown, leaving an unresolved mystery lingering over the recent events.

As a tribute, the three dragonlets created a magnificent museum dedicated to their journey and the works of the legendary designers. This museum was a beacon of inspiration, filled with vibrant exhibits that showcased the evolution of design in Draconia. The Compass and the Palette were meticulously displayed, surrounded by interactive installations that allowed future designers to learn all about the creative process. However, Draco couldn't part with the Ring of Aqureil just yet. Though it was meant to be displayed alongside the other relics, he still wore it, feeling a deep connection to its power and significance. The walls were adorned with masterpieces that seamlessly blended magic and artistry, serving as a testament to the power of imagination.

The Design Council, recognizing the dragonlets' extraordinary contributions, offered them seats on the council itself as specialist advisors. Their insights and experiences were invaluable, shaping the future of Draconian design and ensuring that creativity would always flourish.

But it wasn't enough.

"At least we got to have an adventure before school starts," Arka said as they walked along the walls of the museum.

"Yes, but it doesn't feel like we have done enough to spread the word about the legendary designers. What do you think, Lumi?" asked Draco. He was looking down at Aqureil's ring. It had come to him when he needed it and had won the battle against Celestia. It didn't glow as before, but Draco knew that if he found himself in trouble or needed help, it would be there.

Lumi wasn't paying much attention, "I think that I am hungry!" She patted her stomach.

"You're always hungry!" Arka laughed. "How is your dad doing in his new job, Draco?"

Ignisar assumed the mantle of Chief Executive Officer at Flametail Design with determination and vision. Under his leadership, the studio saw a wave of positive changes. Ignisar championed an inclusive environment where every designer's voice was heard, and everyone had the opportunity to contribute creatively. His commitment to fostering a collaborative and supportive workplace ensured that innovation flourished and each team member felt valued.

The hidden caverns and worlds below the building had been used to help bring in more work for the dragons of Draconia, with each area being cleared, books restored to their former places, and all traps had been removed.

"He is loving it. I have never seen him so happy. Plus, we get to spend more time together, even though he has a lot of important work to do. I like having him around more." Draco said, smiling.

"That's great, Draco." Lumi said. From somewhere she had grabbed a bagel and was taking large bites.

"Just going back to what you said. What do you mean that it isn't enough to spread the word about graphic design?" said Arka.

"I just feel like we each have all this design knowledge. Why not share it with others? Design and creativity have been restored to Draconia. Why don't we spread the word further?" Draco said.

"What if we wrote our own book on design?" Lumi exclaimed.

Arka and Draco looked at each other, smiling.

"That's a great idea, Lumi!" Arka said.

"Yes! Let's see if my dad can help us. Maybe he could even get it published!" Draco said.

The three friends made their way to the Flametail Design building. It seemed brighter than before, exuding a sort of light, even though nothing had changed physically. Despite all the changes that had happened inside.

Misty, the blue fairy, floated to meet them in reception. She now worked in the building, with Draco's dad, to help where she could on projects for the future. The Midnight Shadows were there too. Ignisar had offered them jobs, which they had accepted now that Celestia was gone.

The trio of friends waved at the Midnight Shadows, who were busy working at their desks.

"Misty! So good to see you again! Can we see my dad for a moment, please?" Draco asked.

"Sure, wait here and I shall get him for you." Misty floated away upstairs and soon came down with Ignisar.

"Kids! It's great to see you. What are you doing here, though? I thought you would have spent enough time as it is below these floors..." Ignisar gave the three friends a hug. He looked happier, not as stressed and overworked as before.

"Dad, we want to write a book about what we've learned about graphic design to spread the word about the legends of design, too. What do you think?" Draco said.

Ignisar smiled. "What a great idea! Will you have enough time to complete it before school starts?"

"Yes! We will work hard to complete it and fill the book with everything we have learned!" Arka said.

"Plus, we can keep our strength up with plenty of snacks..." Lumi smiled.

Ignisar laughed. "Of course, plenty of snacks and drinks sounds great to me. What will you call this book? Do you have a title for it yet?"

The three friends exchanged glances, and Draco spoke up, breaking the silence. "How about The Dragon's Guide To Graphic Design?"

After a moment of shared understanding and determination, Draco and his friends knew what they had to do. They exchanged determined nods, ready to tackle the challenges ahead.

As they made their plans, Draco found a quiet moment to himself. He stepped outside the Flametail Design building, the excitement of their new project still buzzing in his mind. But as he looked up at the sky, something lingered at the edge of his thoughts—a presence that had been with him since the start of all of this.

Then, softly at first but growing in strength, the Guardian's voice filled his mind once more, familiar yet different.

"YOU HAVE DONE WELL, DRAGONLET."

Draco paused, recognizing the voice that had guided them through every challenge. But now, standing in the light of their victory, he finally understood.

"YOU'Ve kNOwN me all along," the voice said, gradually shifting from a blend of echoes to a single, clear tone. It was Paula's voice, filled with warmth and pride. "I am Paula Scher. While your journey may be over, the true work is just beginning. Together, we will create a legacy that will inspire generations to come."

Draco's heart swelled with pride as the realization settled in. The voice that had shaped their journey, the wisdom that had guided them—it was her. The legendary designer had been with them every step of the way, and now she would continue to be their guide, not as a distant figure, but as an active mentor and friend.

"I'll see you at the council, Draco," Paula's voice added, a smile in her tone, before the presence faded into the air.

Draco smiled to himself, feeling a surge of excitement for the future. He turned back to join his friends, the knowledge of who the Guardian truly was now a part of him, forever.

So, they threw themselves into their work, using the last few weeks of the school holidays to pour everything they had learned from their adventures into their designs. It was tough at times, but they kept each other's spirits high, working together as friends and making sure each piece honored the four legendary designers who had taught them so much.

Their book, *The Dragon's Guide to Graphic Design*, published by Flametail Design, became an instant best-seller. The friends eagerly promoted the stories and teachings of the design legends, always striving to improve their own skills. They also cherished the friendships they had forged, bonds that would last a lifetime. They had shared an adventure like no other, facing puzzles, enemies, and exploring worlds unseen by anyone else.

Their journey had taught them not only about the power of design but also about the strength of friendship. Their bond as creatives, individuals, and brave warriors in the world of design had profoundly transformed their lives, leaving them with a deeper understanding of what truly mattered. Reflecting on their adventure, they realized they had only begun to uncover the mysteries of Draconia.

This realm, shrouded in secrecy and protected by ancient magic, remained hidden from the prying eyes of outsiders. The magic was so subtle and pervasive that even Draconia's own residents were unaware of its existence, living their lives oblivious to the protective enchantments that shielded their land from the outside world. Though they had ventured to other realms, the young dragons knew they still had much to learn about their own world and the secrets lying beneath its seemingly tranquil surface.

Epilogue
Seeds of Vengeance

Banished from the vibrant world they once knew, Celestia and Grocklepot emerged from the shadows, finding themselves in the heart of the Dull Library. This immense, eerie hall, stretching as far as the eye could see, was lined with towering shelves of blank, colorless books. The air was stale, filled with the scent of old parchment and dust, while the oppressive silence pressed in on them from all sides. In stark contrast to the vibrant world they had been banished from, their new surroundings felt overwhelmingly desolate.

Celestia found herself tasked with the futile job of cataloging these empty tomes, while Grocklepot, always eager to be helpful, attempted to organize the already sorted shelves. "This place is a mind-numbing abyss," Celestia muttered, flipping through yet another blank book. "No inspiration, no creativity—just endless gray."

Grocklepot, always trying to find the silver lining, approached her with a peculiar object. "Ms. Celestia, look what I found! It's an old feather. I don't know why, but it feels... different," he said, his eyes wide with a mix of curiosity and excitement.

Celestia stared at the feather skeptically, dismissing it as just another dull artifact from this dreary place. "Another useless relic in this wasteland," she grumbled, taking the feather from Grocklepot. But as she held it, the feather transformed within her claws, revealing itself as the Quill of Typographus, glowing with a faint, mystical light.

Celestia's eyes widened in realization. "Grocklepot, where did you find this?"

Grocklepot grinned, pleased with himself. "I, uh, found it in that stormy world with the giant sketchbook. It was sitting on a pedestal, and I thought it might be useful someday, so I swapped it with a regular quill," he explained, unaware of the gravity of his actions.

Celestia's eyes narrowed, both impressed and irritated. "You bumbling fool," she muttered, half in frustration, half in admiration. "This quill could be our key to escape!" She could hardly believe it—the Quill of Typographus, capable of bringing words and designs to life, had been in their possession all along.

As she held the Quill of Typographus, a gleam of triumph flickered in Celestia's eyes. The realization of what she possessed sent a thrill through her—this powerful relic was the key to escaping the Dull Library. Finally, a chance to break free and reclaim her place in Draconia. She couldn't help but cackle, the sound echoing ominously in the quiet library. Grocklepot, oblivious to the gravity of the situation, joined in with a giggle, pleased that his surprise had seemingly delighted his mistress.

As Celestia contemplated her next move, a sinister smile spread across her face. The power to reshape her fate—and that of Draconia—was now in her claws.

THE END?

Real Life Design Legends
Meet Gail Anderson

Gail Anderson is a distinguished graphic designer, writer, and educator based in New York City. Born in 1962 in the Bronx, she developed an early interest in design through handmade magazines inspired by popular culture. Anderson graduated from the School of Visual Arts (SVA) in 1984 with a degree in Media Arts.

Her career took off at Rolling Stone, where she worked for fifteen years, becoming the senior art director and defining the magazine's visual style with her innovative typography. After Rolling Stone, Anderson joined SpotCo, a leading entertainment design agency, creating iconic artwork for Broadway shows. Currently, she serves as the creative director at Visual Arts Press at SVA and is a partner at Anderson Newton Design, a multi-disciplinary design firm.

Design Philosophy and Notable Works

Gail Anderson's work is renowned for its bold, typography-driven designs. She emphasizes collaboration and draws inspiration from her students and everyday experiences. Her design philosophy centers on communication through design, creating visually engaging and meaningful work.

Among her notable projects is the design of the USPS stamp commemorating the 150th anniversary of the Emancipation Proclamation, which sold over 50 million copies. Gail also designed a series of posters for the School of the Visual Arts, incorporating her love for typography into the identity. Her work spans various media, including book covers, posters, and postage stamps, often addressing social and political issues.

Recognition and Contributions

Gail Anderson has received numerous accolades, including the National Design Award for Lifetime Achievement from the Cooper Hewitt, Smithsonian Design Museum in 2018, and an honorary doctorate from Pennsylvania College of Art & Design. She is a passionate advocate for diversity in the design industry, encouraging young designers, particularly those of color, to pursue their ambitions despite challenges. Anderson believes in the importance of mentorship and has dedicated much of her career to teaching and inspiring the next generation of designers.

USPS Stamp Commemorating The 150th Anniversary of the Emancipation Proclamation

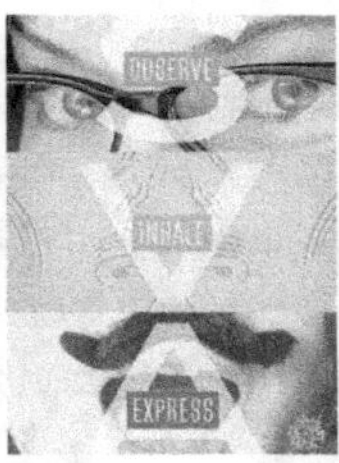

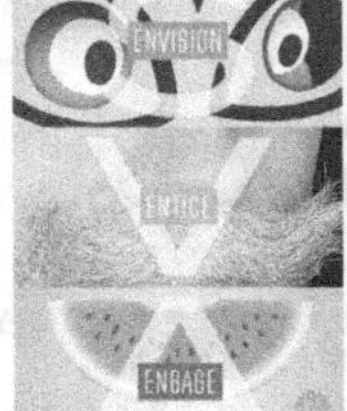

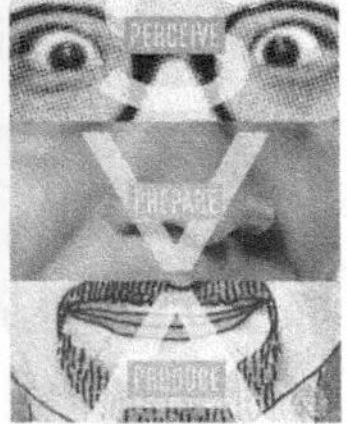

Posters for The School of the Visual Arts

Rolling Stone Magazine

Gail's Personal Bottlecap Collection

Real Life Design Legends

Meet Chip Kidd

Chip Kidd, born on September 12, 1964, in Reading, Pennsylvania, is a renowned graphic designer best known for his innovative book cover designs. After graduating from Pennsylvania State University with a degree in graphic design, Kidd began his career at Alfred A. Knopf in 1986, where he currently serves as V.P. Art Director and Editor At-Large. Over his career, he has designed more than 1,500 book covers for authors such as Michael Crichton, Haruki Murakami, and David Sedaris.

Kidd's work is characterized by his refusal to adopt a singular style, instead tailoring each design to the book's content. His approach is deeply conceptual, aiming to create covers that encapsulate the essence of the book's narrative.

Design Philosophy and Notable Works

Chip Kidd's design philosophy revolves around communication through simplicity and clarity. He believes that effective design solutions come from understanding the subject matter and a commitment to experimentation. His work is marked by a playful yet profound approach to design, often incorporating elements of surprise and wit.

One of Kidd's most iconic designs is the cover for Michael Crichton's Jurassic Park, featuring the silhouetted T. rex skeleton. This design became a cultural touchstone and remains one of the most recognizable book covers in modern publishing history. Another significant work is his book Go: A Kidd's Guide to Graphic Design, which introduces young readers to the fundamentals of graphic design through engaging and interactive content.

Recognition and Contributions

Chip Kidd has received numerous accolades, including the AIGA Medal in 2014 and the National Design Award for Communication in 2007. He is also known for his engaging public speaking and contributions to design education. Kidd's TED talks are celebrated for their humor and insight, making design accessible and intriguing to a broad audience.

In addition to his design work, Kidd is an accomplished author. His books, such as The Cheese Monkeys and The Learners, explore the intersections of design and storytelling. Through his prolific career, Kidd has significantly influenced the field of graphic design, demonstrating the power of a well-designed book cover to communicate and captivate.

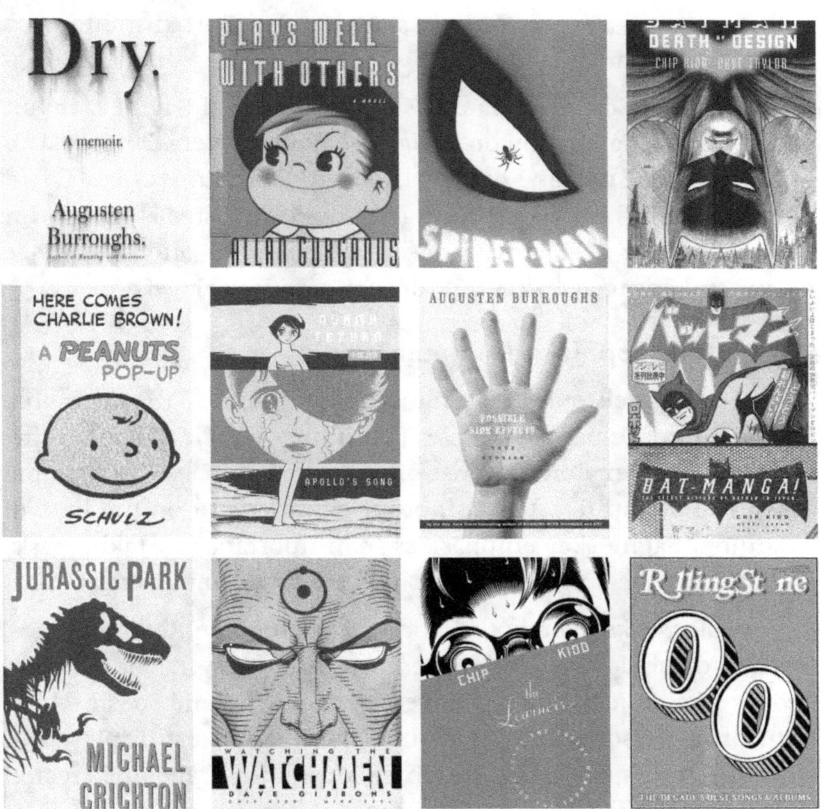

A Variety of Book Covers from Chip Kidd's Portfolio

Real Life Design Legends

Meet Stefan Sagmeister

Stefan Sagmeister, born on August 6, 1962, in Austria, is a renowned graphic designer and typographer based in New York City. He co-founded the influential design firm Sagmeister & Walsh with Jessica Walsh in 2012. Sagmeister's career began in Austria, where he worked for a youth magazine before moving to New York to study at the Pratt Institute on a Fulbright scholarship.

Sagmeister's career took off when he founded Sagmeister Inc. in 1993, focusing initially on designing album covers. His work for musical artists such as Lou Reed, The Rolling Stones, and David Byrne brought him widespread acclaim. Sagmeister is known for his unorthodox and provocative designs, which often challenge norms and engage viewers on a deeper emotional level.

Design Philosophy and Notable Works

Stefan Sagmeister's design philosophy centers on the belief that design can make people happier and improve their quality of life. His work often explores themes of happiness and beauty, blending art with thoughtful, often humorous commentary on the human condition. Sagmeister emphasizes the importance of taking risks and pursuing personal projects to fuel creativity and innovation.

Notable works include the album cover for The Rolling Stones' Bridges to Babylon, which features an intricate Assyrian lion design, and his own project, Things I Have Learned in My Life So Far, which transforms personal reflections into typographic art displayed in various public spaces. His multimedia exhibition, Beauty, created with Jessica Walsh, explores the impact of beauty on our daily lives through diverse mediums such as product design, architecture, and city planning.

Recognition and Contributions

Sagmeister has been recognized with numerous awards, including several Grammy Awards for his album designs and the National Design Award. He is celebrated for his contributions to the field of graphic design, not only for his commercial work but also for his self-initiated projects that challenge traditional design boundaries and encourage reflection on broader societal issues.

Rolling Stones Bridges to Babylon

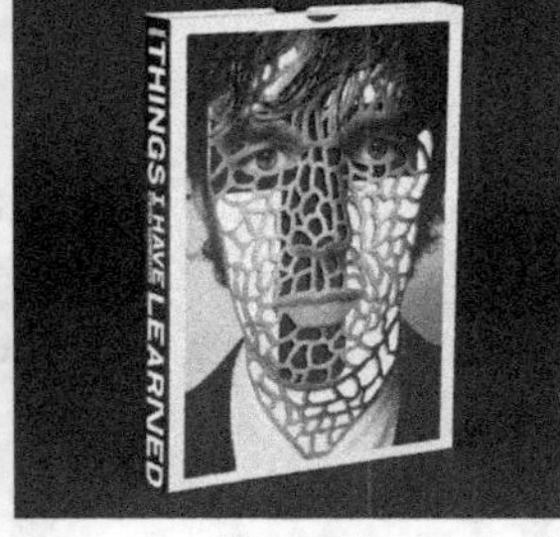

Beautiful Numbers

Things I've Learned in My Life So Far

Beautification

Real Life Design Legends
Meet Paula Scher

Paula Scher, born on October 6, 1948, in Washington, D.C., is a distinguished American graphic designer, painter, and educator. She began her career after earning a Bachelor of Fine Arts from the Tyler School of Art in 1970. Scher made her mark in the record industry, creating iconic album covers for both Atlantic and CBS Records in the 1970s. She joined Pentagram as the first female principal in 1991, where she has worked on identity systems, environmental graphics, packaging, and publication designs for a wide range of high-profile clients.

Design Philosophy and Notable Works

Paula Scher is known for her bold, expressive style and innovative use of typography. Her design philosophy centers on the idea that great design comes from obsession and a deep understanding of the subject matter. She believes in fast, instinctive creative processes, often allowing room for mistakes to lead to unique and interesting results.

Scher's most notable works include the visual identity for The Public Theater in New York City, which she developed in 1994. This design has become a landmark in theatrical promotion and is recognized for its use of bold, vibrant typography that mimics street art. Another significant project is the redesign of the Citibank logo in 1998, which helped modernize and unify the bank's global identity. Her work for The High Line, a public park in New York City, showcases her ability to blend industrial aesthetics with modern design.

** Photo credit: Christopher Garcia Valle*

Recognition and Contributions

Throughout her illustrious career, Paula Scher has received numerous accolades, including the AIGA Medal in 2001, the National Design Award for Communication Design in 2013, and the Royal Designer for Industry in 2021. Her work is exhibited in major museums, such as the Museum of Modern Art and the Cooper Hewitt, Smithsonian Design Museum. Scher is also an influential educator, having taught at institutions like the School of Visual Arts and Yale University. Her contributions to the field of graphic design continue to inspire and influence new generations of designers.

The Public Theater Promotional Design

citibank

Citibank Logo Design

The High Line Public Park Environmental Design

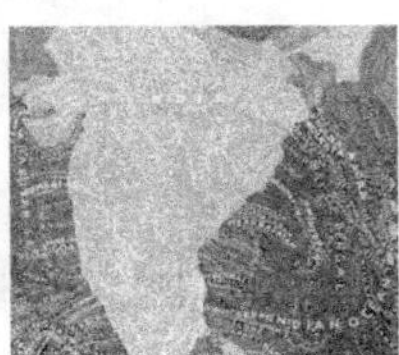

Series of Handpainted Maps

Draco's Design Challenges

Welcome to The Creative Process

Hey there, fellow adventurers! It's me, Draco, and I'm so excited to welcome you to a journey through the magical world of design. Just like in Draconia, where creativity and magic blend to create something extraordinary, you're about to embark on a quest of your own—the quest of design! Whether you're crafting a logo for Flametail Design or hunting down the perfect layout for a poster, you'll need to tap into your creativity, imagination, and problem-solving skills.

In Draconia, we don't just wing it (well, sometimes we do, but only when we're flying!). We follow a process—a way of thinking and creating that helps us turn our ideas into something real and blazing! **So, don't skip any steps or mix up the order**—they all matter. Ready to dive in? Let's go!

1. Inspiration and Research to Gather Your Spark

- **Why it matters:** Before you start designing, it's important to know what your design is supposed to do. Understanding who it's for and what it needs to say will guide your ideas and make your design stronger.
- **How to do it:** Look at examples of similar designs to get ideas. Think about what makes them work and how they connect to what you want to create.

2. Idea Generation to Let Your Imagination Soar

- **Why It Matters:** This is where you brainstorm. Let your imagination run wild! The goal is to come up with as many ideas as possible. There are no bad ideas in this stage. All are welcome.
- **How to do it:** Sketch out quick ideas, make lists, or even jot down words that come to mind. Don't worry about getting it perfect at this stage—just focus on exploring different possibilities.

3. Concept Development to Forge Your Best Concept

- **Why It Matters:** Out of all those ideas, which one shines the brightest? Choose the ones that fit your goal best and start refining them.
- **How to do it:** Take your favorite ideas and start developing them into strong concepts. Think about how they could work as finished designs. Make sure they're clear and aligned with the purpose you set out in the first step.

4. Design & Execution to Bring It to Life

- **Why It Matters:** Here's where the real magic happens! Turn your ideas into actual designs.
- **How to do it:** Create your design with care, paying attention to details like colors, fonts, and layout. Make sure it's clear, easy to understand, and looks as awesome as you imagined. Think about how your design will work in the real world—like how a logo might look on a sign or how a poster will catch someone's eye.

5. Feedback & Refinement will Get Some Dragon Eyes on It

- **Why It Matters:** Even the best dragons need a second pair of eyes! Feedback helps you see things you might have missed.
- **How to do it:** Share your design with friends, family, or fellow dragons and listen to their thoughts. Use their feedback to make your design even better. Sometimes that means going back and making changes, but that's all part of the process.

6. Finalization & Presentation to Show It to the World

- **Why It Matters:** You're almost there! Now it's time to make sure your design is polished and ready to share.
- **How to do it:** Add the finishing touches, making sure everything looks just right. Then, prepare to present your work to others. Think about how you can best showcase your design—whether it's a mock-up or a full presentation, let your work shine!

Your Quest Awaits!

Draco's Design Challenges

Project One

A new logo for Flametail Design

Creative Brief

You've been selected to create a logo for Flametail Design, one of Draconia's most respected design firms. Flametail Design is renowned for its innovative and magical approach to graphic design, combining creativity with a touch of fantasy to produce stunning visual solutions. Your task is to design a logo that reflects the company's core values of innovation, professionalism, and creativity, while also capturing the essence of Draconia—a world where dragons and magic play a central role.

Objectives

- **Innovation:** The logo should feel modern and forward-thinking, representing Flametail Design's reputation for cutting-edge design.
- **Professionalism:** The logo needs to convey a sense of trust and reliability, making it suitable for business cards, signage, and digital platforms.
- **Creativity and Fantasy:** Incorporate elements that hint at the magical world of Draconia, such as a flame or tail motif, while keeping the design clean and simple.

Target Audience:

The logo should appeal to a diverse audience, including business clients looking for creative solutions, potential employees who are passionate about design, and the wider Draconian community who admire Flametail's work.

Tone and Style:

The tone of the logo should be bold, creative, and professional. It should stand out but also be versatile enough to work in various formats and sizes. Consider using symbolism that connects to Draconia's rich culture, such as a dragon's tail, fire, or mystical symbols, but ensure it remains elegant and not overly complex.

Unlock Your Best Design:

Follow the Creative Process from start to finish.

1. Inspiration & Research:

- Look at logos from other design firms for inspiration. Think about symbols that represent Flametail Design, such as flames or dragon tails, and consider how to incorporate them creatively into your design.

2. Idea Generation:

- Sketch 5-10 quick ideas for the logo, experimenting with different symbols, fonts, and layouts. Focus on keeping the designs simple, memorable, and reflective of Flametail Design's identity.

3. Concept Development:

- Choose the sketch that best captures the essence of Flametail Design and refine the drawing making adjustments to improve balance and readability.

4. Design & Execution:

- Add color, experimenting with different color combinations that work with the brand's creative and professional vibe. Ensure the logo looks polished and suitable for various applications like business cards, signage, and digital media.

5. Feedback & Refinement:

- Share your logo design with a peer or mentor to get constructive feedback. Use their suggestions to refine your design, making it stronger and more effective.

6. Finalization & Presentation:

- Finalize your logo, ensuring it is balanced, clear, and visually appealing.

7. Deliver your work:

- Present your final logo to a peer, teacher, or mentor.
- Submit your work to Draco's Design Challenges at www.TheDragonCodexBK.com

Draco's Design Challenges

Project Two

A poster for the Grand Design Contest

Creative Brief

You've been tasked with designing a poster to promote the Grand Design Contest, the most prestigious competition hosted by the Everbright Design Council in Draconia. This contest invites young dragons to showcase their creativity by creating a map of Draconia that is both artistic and functional. Your poster needs to capture the attention of potential contestants, inspire them to participate, and clearly convey all the essential details about the contest.

Objectives

- **Attention-Grabbing:** The poster needs to be visually striking to catch the eye of young dragons and make them excited about entering the contest.
- **Informative:** Clearly communicate the contest's theme, entry deadline, prize information, and how to submit entries.
- **Inspirational:** The design should inspire young dragons to unleash their creativity and participate, showing that this is a chance to be part of something big.

Target Audience:

The primary audience for this poster is young dragons, aged 12-18, who have an interest in art and design. However, it should also appeal to their mentors, teachers, and families, who might encourage them to enter the contest.

Tone and Style:

The poster should have a vibrant, energetic, and creative tone, using colors and imagery that reflect the adventurous spirit of the contest. Consider incorporating elements of map-making (such as compasses, grids, and landmarks) and blending them with Draconian themes like dragons, magical symbols, and fantasy landscapes. The overall design should feel inviting and accessible, making young dragons eager to join the contest.

Unlock Your Best Design:

Follow the Creative Process from start to finish.

1. Inspiration & Research:

- Review the contest details, including the theme, deadline, and prizes. Look at examples of posters that effectively convey important information while being visually appealing.

2. Idea Generation:

- Sketch a few layout ideas for the poster, considering how to best organize the title, contest details, and images. Think about using symbols and visuals related to the contest theme, such as maps, dragons, or design tools

3. Concept Development:

- Select the layout that works best for communicating the contest information clearly and engagingly. Develop your chosen concept, refining the position of text and images to ensure the poster is eye-catching and easy to understand.

4. Design & Execution:

- Create your poster, adding bright, vibrant colors that make the design stand out. Ensure that the headline is bold and that all important details are easy to read at a glance.

5. Feedback & Refinement:

- Share your poster design with a peer or mentor to receive feedback on its effectiveness. Refine your design based on their input, improving any areas that need more clarity or visual impact.
- Finalize the poster by making sure all elements are balanced and the information is clear.

6. Deliver your work:

- Present your final logo to a peer, teacher, or mentor.
- Submit your work to Draco's Design Challenges at www.TheDragonCodexBK.com

Draco's Design Challenges

Project Three

A new book cover design for "The Codex of Design"

Creative Brief

Imagine that you've been asked to design the book cover for a new edition of the "Codex of Design," a legendary book that holds the secrets of design in Draconia. Your challenge is to create a cover that captures the essence of this magical and powerful book. The cover should be visually striking, blending fantasy elements with design symbolism, making it a must-have for every dragon in Draconia.

Objectives

- **Magical and Mysterious:** The cover should evoke a sense of mystery and magic, reflecting the hidden knowledge within the book.
- **Timeless and Elegant:** The design should feel timeless, as if it has been passed down through generations, while still being elegant and appealing to modern readers.
- **Symbolic:** Incorporate symbols of design (like compasses, quills, or palettes) that connect with the themes of creativity and mastery.

Target Audience:

The cover should appeal to dragons of all ages who are passionate about design, especially those who are curious about the ancient secrets of the craft. It should intrigue both seasoned designers and young students eager to learn.

Tone and Style:

The tone should be mysterious, magical, and elegant. Use rich colors, intricate details, and fantasy-inspired fonts to create a cover that feels both ancient and powerful. Consider adding ornate borders, mystical symbols, and a central image that represents the Codex's importance.

Unlock Your Best Design:

Follow the Creative Process from start to finish.

1. Inspiration & Research:

- Research book covers that blend fantasy and design elements for inspiration. Think about how to incorporate magical symbols, rich colors, and elegant typography that reflect the Codex's legendary status.

2. Idea Generation:

- Sketch 2-3 quick cover designs, exploring different ways to arrange the title, central image, and decorative elements. Experiment with symbols of magic and design, such as glowing effects, ancient runes, or a mystical central image.

3. Concept Development:

- Choose the cover design that best represents the mystery and power of the Codex. Develop your chosen concept, adding more detail and refining the layout to create a cohesive and striking design.

4. Design & Execution:

- Add color and detail to your cover, using a rich color palette that evokes a sense of magic and mystery. Incorporate intricate borders, symbols, and textures to give the cover an ancient and valuable feel.

5. Feedback & Refinement:

- Share your book cover design with a peer or mentor to gather feedback on its effectiveness and visual appeal. Use their suggestions to refine your design, focusing on enhancing the cover's impact and cohesiveness.

6. Finalization & Presentation:

- Finalize the book cover, ensuring that all elements are well-balanced and the design is visually compelling.

7. Deliver your work:

- Present your final logo to a peer, teacher, or mentor.
- Submit your work to Draco's Design Challenges at www.TheDragonCodexBK.com

Glossary

Design Terminology

Art Gallery
A dedicated space for exhibiting and selling artworks. In the context of graphic design, art galleries may showcase a variety of visual works such as posters, illustrations, and digital art, often highlighting innovative design techniques and trends.

Art History: Art Deco
A style of visual arts, architecture, and design that first appeared in France just before World War I. Art Deco combines modernist styles with fine craftsmanship and rich materials. It is characterized by bold geometric patterns, vibrant colors, and intricate details. For example, the Chrysler Building in New York is a famous example of Art Deco architecture.

Art History: Art Nouveau
An international style of art, architecture, and applied art, especially the decorative arts, that was most popular between 1890 and 1910. Art Nouveau is characterized by its use of long, sinuous, organic lines and was employed most often in architecture, interior design, jewelry, and glass design. Think of the flowing lines of Alphonse Mucha's posters.

Art History: Bauhaus
A German art school operational from 1919 to 1933 that combined crafts and the fine arts. The Bauhaus aimed to reunite fine art and functional design, creating practical objects with the soul of artworks. The style is characterized by its focus on simplicity, functionality, and the use of modern materials. Bauhaus buildings often have a sleek, minimalistic look.

Art History: Cubism
An early 20th-century art movement led by Pablo Picasso and Georges Braque, characterized by fragmented objects and multiple perspectives within a single plane. Cubism breaks subjects into geometric shapes and depicts them from various angles. For example, Picasso's painting "Les Demoiselles d'Avignon" is a famous Cubist work.

Art History: Impressionism
Originating in the late 19th century, characterized by small, thin brush strokes, open composition, and an emphasis on accurate depiction of light. Often capture the feeling of a scene rather than the details. Examples include works by Claude Monet.

Art History: Modernism
A broad movement in Western arts and literature that gathered pace from around 1850, characterized by a deliberate departure from tradition and the use of innovative forms of expression. In graphic design, modernism favors clean lines, a lack of clutter, and the use of sans-serif fonts. Examples include the works of designers like Paul Rand.

Art History: Surrealism
A 20th-century avant-garde movement in art and literature that sought to release the creative potential of the unconscious mind, often through bizarre, dream-like imagery. Salvador Dalí's paintings are iconic examples of surrealism.

Art Techniques
A broad range of methods and processes used in creating artworks. This includes traditional techniques like drawing, painting, and sculpting, as well as modern methods such as digital illustration and 3D modeling. Mastery of these techniques allows artists to express their creativity effectively.

Baseline
The imaginary line upon which most letters in a typeface sit. The baseline is crucial in typography as it ensures consistency and readability. Descenders, such as those in the letters "g" and "y," extend below this line.

Branding
The process of creating a unique image, name, and identity for a product or service in the consumer's mind, primarily through advertising campaigns with a consistent theme. Effective branding helps to establish a significant and differentiated presence in the market that attracts and retains loyal customers. An example is the Nike "swoosh" logo.

Contrast
The difference in luminance, color, or texture that makes an object distinguishable from others within the same field of view. High contrast can draw attention and create visual interest, while low contrast can create a more subtle and cohesive look. Black text on a white background is a high contrast combination.

Creative Process
The iterative journey of developing a creative work. This process typically involves stages such as brainstorming, research, sketching, prototyping, and refining ideas. Each step is crucial for generating innovative and well-thought-out designs. Think of designing a new logo, starting from rough sketches to the final polished version.

Design Contest
A structured competition where participants submit designs based on specific criteria or themes. These contests are often used to recognize and reward creative talent, providing designers with opportunities to showcase their skills and gain visibility.

Design Principles
Fundamental guidelines that help designers create visually appealing and functional compositions. Key principles include balance, contrast, emphasis, hierarchy, movement, pattern, rhythm, and unity. These principles ensure that a design is both aesthetically pleasing and effectively communicates its intended message.

Golden Ratio
A mathematical ratio, approximately 1.618 to 1, found in nature and art. It is used in design to create harmonious and aesthetically pleasing compositions. The golden ratio can be applied to layout, spacing, and proportions within a design to achieve a balanced and natural look. For example, many classical buildings and artworks use the golden ratio in their proportions.

Graphic Design
The art and practice of planning and projecting ideas and experiences with visual and textual content. This involves the application of color theory, typography, composition, and design software to create visual content that communicates messages effectively.

Hierarchy
In design, hierarchy refers to the arrangement and presentation of elements in order of importance. This concept helps guide the viewer's eye through the content, ensuring that the most important information is noticed first. Techniques to establish hierarchy include size, color, contrast, and placement.

Kerning
The process of adjusting the spacing between individual characters in a font to achieve a visually pleasing result. Proper kerning improves the readability and overall appearance of text by ensuring consistent and aesthetically balanced spacing.

Layout Design
The arrangement of visual elements on a page. Good layout design enhances the readability and effectiveness of the displayed information. It involves organizing text, images, and other content in a coherent and aesthetically pleasing manner.

Leading
(pronounced "ledding") The vertical distance between the baselines of successive lines of type. Proper leading ensures readability and aesthetic appeal in typography by providing adequate spacing between lines of text.

Portfolio
A collection of a designer's work showcasing their skills, creativity, and range. Used to demonstrate abilities to potential clients or employers. For example, a graphic designer might include samples of logos, posters, and website designs in their portfolio.

Rule of Thirds
A design principle that divides an image into nine equal parts, using two equally spaced horizontal lines and two equally spaced vertical lines. The key elements in the design are placed along these lines or at their intersections to create balance and interest. Photographers often use the rule of thirds to compose their shots.

Tracking
The process of adjusting the overall spacing between letters in a block of text. This differs from kerning, which adjusts spacing between specific letter pairs. Proper tracking ensures that the text is evenly spaced and readable, preventing it from looking too tight or too loose.

Typography
The art and technique of arranging type to make written language legible, readable, and visually appealing. Includes the selection of typefaces, point sizes, line lengths, line-spacing, and letter-spacing.

Glossary

Lumi's Color Wheel

Color Theory

Color theory is the guide that helps us understand how colors work together. It's like a map that shows which colors look good together and how they affect our feelings and designs.

Complementary color harmony

Complementary colors are two colors that are opposite each other on the color wheel. When placed next to each other, they make each other stand out, creating a strong contrast.

Split Complementary color harmony

Split complementary is like a twist on complementary colors. Instead of using the color directly opposite, you use the two colors next to it. This gives you three colors that work well together, with a little more variety.

Triadic color harmony

A triadic color scheme uses three colors that are evenly spaced on the color wheel. These colors create a balanced and vibrant look because they are different from each other but still work together.

Tetradic color harmony

Tetradic is a color scheme that uses four colors, forming a rectangle on the color wheel. It gives you lots of color options, but you need to balance them well to avoid overwhelming your design.

Analogous color harmony

Analogous colors are neighbors on the color wheel. They are next to each other and usually look nice together because they have similar tones, creating a calm and easy-on-the-eyes look.

Monochromatic color harmony

Monochromatic colors are all different shades, tints, and tones of the same color. It's like taking one color and playing with how light or dark it is to create a simple but unified design.

Primary Colors

Primary colors are the three basic colors that can't be made by mixing other colors together. They are red, blue, and yellow. These colors are like the building blocks for all the other colors. When you mix primary colors, you can create new colors!

Secondary Colors

Secondary colors are made by mixing two primary colors together. For example, if you mix red and blue, you get purple. Mix blue and yellow, and you get green. Mix yellow and red, and you get orange. These colors are one step away from the primary colors and help expand the color palette.

Tertiary Colors

Tertiary colors are created by mixing a primary color with a secondary color next to it on the color wheel. This gives you colors like red-orange, yellow-green, and blue-purple. Tertiary colors add even more variety to your color choices, giving you a wider range of options for your designs.

Acknowledgments
Thank you!

First and foremost, to my family—Dana, Spencer, Tyler, Mom, Dad, and of course, Jordan—thank you for your unconditional support and encouragement. This book was created with you in mind. **Family is everything!**

I would like to begin by thanking Alex Sordi for her valuable support at the start of this project. Her early contributions helped lay the groundwork for this book.

I would also like to thank my editor, Matthew Greenacre, whose exceptional writing skills and dedication were pivotal in bringing this book to life. He stepped in when I needed him most, transforming the narrative into a cohesive and compelling story. Thank you, Matthew, for your invaluable contribution and for helping me realize my dream.

My heartfelt thanks goes to Abby Watson, whose beautiful cover illustration has breathed life into the world of dragons. Your creativity and talent have added a magical touch to this book, making the story even more enchanting.

And, I am sincerely thankful for receiving personal notes of approval from four of my design heroes, Paula Scher, Stefan Sagmeister, Gail Anderson, and Chip Kidd, to include each of them in this story. It is my intention to illuminate and celebrate these legendary designers and to educate the world about their influence and contributions.

Finally, thank YOU for taking your precious time to read "The Dragon Codex: Quest for the Relics of Design." Without you, the world of Draconia couldn't possibly come alive. I hope you've enjoyed the story of Draco, Lumi and Arka in their creative quests.

About the Author
David Block
Graphic Designer, Educator

David Block is a long-time graphic designer with over 30 years of experience. His journey into the world of design began in 1991 at a Southern California mall kiosk, where he first used Adobe Photoshop 2.0 to create personalized mugs and t-shirts.

This initial encounter sparked a lifelong passion, leading him to earn a Bachelor's in Graphic Design from The Art Institute of California—Orange County. Throughout his career, David has worked across various industries, bringing creativity and innovation to each project.

In 2015, David shifted his focus to education, as a teacher with North Orange County ROP, developing the Graphic Design pathway in the Digital Media Arts Academy at El Dorado High School. In 2018, he established the 'Design Rescue Studio,' a work based learning program that merges academic learning with real world design projects, providing students with practical experience. Additionally, David launched 'The Design Rescue Show' on YouTube to inspire and educate aspiring designers worldwide.

David's dedication to nurturing creativity and innovation in young minds, combined with his extensive professional background, uniquely positions him to author "The Dragon Codex: Quest for the Relics of Design," a book aimed at inspiring the next generation of graphic designers.

Visit TheDragonCodexBK.com to learn more.

If you have feedback, I'd love to hear it! Please consider leaving a review.

www.ingramcontent.com/pod-product-compliance
Lightning Source LLC
Chambersburg PA
CBHW071430260626

47170CB00008B/2657
9798218981563